THE SLIP THROUGH TIME

ADULT FICTION BY THE AUTHOR

Dear Kate—Dear Dad,
The Isle across Acheron

DENALI MAJESTO'S

the SLIP through TIME

To my parents:
—Mom, for cultivating in me a love of books—
—Dad, for teaching me the meaning of adventure—

"Friends are the family we choose for ourselves."
- EDNA BUCHANAN

Chapter One

WHAT HAPPENED IN TIKAL

A GOLDEN THREAD OF SUNLIGHT squeezes through the solitary crack in the stone wall and falls upon Itzel's closed eyelid. The eye beneath quivers back and forth, struggling between a dream and the waking world.

Suddenly, both the raven-haired girl's eyes burst open. She sits upright on her mat and glances around the room.

"Oh, no no no no no!" she moans.

The other mats laid about the floor are empty. The rest of her family has already awoken and begun their day, while she—"lazy little Itzel," as her older brother calls her—has overslept. Again.

And today of all days!

Itzel hurriedly throws her body-length *trajé* over her head. After wrestling to fit the garment around herself properly, she bursts through the woolen curtain that divides the tiny bedroom from the living quarters of the small home.

No one is there. Her fears are confirmed. The others have left for the city of Tikal.

Itzel steps outside into the brilliant sunshine. The cool air promises a more temperate day. This will be a nice break from the sweltering heat of the past weeks. She gazes northward and sees the great stone peaks of Tikal's temples, looming above and beyond the emerald-green jungle canopy. They stand proud, those immovable guardians of both gods and people. They are not far. Perhaps if she leaves now, she can catch up to her family.

"Itzel, my *winchikin*," speaks a low, airy voice behind her.

She whirls about with surprise. The kind, dark eyes and wrinkled brown face of her grandmother are smiling up at her.

"Good morning, *mim*," Itzel replies, bowing her head in respect. Immediately returning to her panicked state, she asks, "Are they all gone? To Tikal?"

The old woman chuckles and says, "Indeed they have, Itzel. Those who desire much sleep miss out on much life. And you, my Itzel, desire sleep more than anyone I have ever known!"

Itzel hangs her head, unable to hide her disappointment. For many nights, since the elders announced the upcoming festival, she has been anxiously waiting to spend the day in Tikal. Itzel loves the busy streets of the city—the excited people, the towering buildings, the vendors in their wooden booths hawking their goods. And what sorts of extra sights and sounds and smells might she experience on a day like today!

But her parents have forbidden her traveling the jungle path to Tikal by herself. Her brother was allowed to make the journey when he was ten years old, but Itzel is only nine. This means she is stuck in her little village of Cuzacal for the day. Instead of street performers and dancers wearing feathered costumes and headdresses, her only company will be Grandmother Xoc.

"Do cheer up, little Itzel," Xoc says, grabbing the girl's hand and patting it gently. "They will return in the afternoon. We will feast together with all of Cuzacal. And then, before the sun goes down, they will bring you to Tikal for the Sunset Celebration."

"Yes, grandmother," murmurs Itzel. She is cheered little by her grandmother's words.

Xoc's affectionate grin widens, and she says, "Your bad luck is my good fortune, as it turns out. I am in great need of two strong, young hands to assist in making tonight's *wa'il*."

Itzel's eyes brighten. *Wa'il*, her grandmother's famous tortillas, have been a family secret for ages. Often the whole village gathers around Grandmother Xoc's *wa'il*, and the people feast until their bellies are full and round.

Xoc doesn't wait for a response. She merely chuckles and motions for Itzel to follow her, exclaiming, "Come with me, my dear *winchikin!* Today you take an important step toward your womanhood! Haha!"

Itzel bows her head as she passes through the low doorway into Grandmother Xoc's home. This hut is smaller than her family's. Her grandfather once lived here when Itzel was very small, but he has been gone a long time. One day he went for a hunt in the jungle and never returned.

"What do you need help with, *mim?*" Itzel asks.

Pointing at a low table containing various clay jars and bowls, Xoc answers, "My ancient bones have lost their strength. I cannot grind the *ixim* for our tortillas as when I was young. Today, the job belongs to you."

Itzel brushes her black hair from her nut-brown face and nods reverently. But in her heart, she wishes more than ever that she could be in Tikal with her family. She silently vows that from now on she will wake even before the roosters.

According to her grandmother's instructions, Itzel uses a smooth stone to mash the *ixim*—the boiled maize—into a pasty dough. When each batch is finished, she and her grandmother roll the dough into fist-sized balls, which they set aside. Later, Grandmother Xoc will cook them over the fire, and the village will eat the tortillas steaming fresh.

As Itzel works, a question arises in her mind, and she asks, "Grandmother? Why *is* there a festival today? It isn't one of our customary celebrations."

"The rumors are flying, of course," Xoc replies from the comfort of her chair. "The most reliable ones claim it is because Kinich Ahau is upset."

"Upset? Why do they think that?" Itzel asks. She doesn't know much about the Sun God, but she is aware that one wouldn't want to upset Kinich Ahau.

Xoc leans forward in her chair, and her eyes narrow. She lowers her tone like one telling a dark secret as she says, "The chiefs who study the sky say the sun has been acting strangely. Some days it is too hot for this time of year. Other days it is too cold. Perhaps Kinich Ahau is heartbroken. Perhaps he is angry. Some even believe it means the gods may come and bring judgment soon."

Itzel holds her breath. She has never seen her grandmother so serious before.

Suddenly, Xoc erupts into more laughter and says, "Or maybe the chiefs are bored and want a party! That answer seems far more likely to me."

Itzel offers a meager grin. Her grandmother never seems to believe much of what the chiefs or shamans tell them. Itzel, on the other hand, wonders if it's possible that the gods will visit during the festival. And, if they did, would they be pleased to bless the city? Or would they find fault with the people of Tikal and punish them?

When Itzel is finished mashing the last of the *ixim,* she sets the small grinding bowl on the table. The dough's earthy aroma is already causing her mouth to water, and the promise of *wa'il* stuffed with fragrant avocados, crunchy chiles, and roasted meat replaces every fear she has about the gods.

A shadow falls across the room. Somebody is standing in the doorway, blocking the sunlight.

"Can Itzel come and play?" a timid voice asks.

The girl turns to see Aapo, the neighbor boy one year younger than her. He spins a ball from side to side in his hands.

"For the moment she is busy helping me," Xoc answers warmly. "But she will be done shortly, and when she is, she may play to her heart's fullness."

"Are you making *wa'il?*" Aapo inquires hopefully, peeking at the dough balls on the table.

Grandmother Xoc winks at him. "You will find out later, boy! Now run along. Itzel will be finished soon."

"What do I still need to do?" Itzel asks, once Aapo has run off.

"The only thing left," Xoc slyly replies, "is the small matter of our most important ingredient!" Then, with a laugh, she adds, "Well, most important besides the tortillas themselves. Haha!"

Her grandmother's infectious mood brings a smile to Itzel's own face. "And what is that?" she asks.

"The *uniwa,* dear granddaughter! The avocados!" exclaims Xoc, pinching her granddaughter's cheeks.

"Where are they?"

"Still on the tree, you silly girl! The ones on the lower branches have been picked already. I need you to scramble up higher to get them for me," Xoc says, thrusting an empty basket into Itzel's hands.

With a girlish giggle, Itzel hurries out the door, carrying the woven basket. The avocado grove lies at the furthest edge of Cuzacal. She doesn't know how long her family has tended the hundreds of handsome trees, only that her grandfather did so before her father— her *yum*. She also knows that their avocados, which grow in the shadow of the great jungle trees, are renowned throughout Tikal as superior to all others.

As she walks, the breeze carries with it the tormenting echoes of the festival in the distance. The cheerful voices of men and women and children, the melodic singing of a dozen voices, the clamoring instruments—they seem to taunt her, as if aware that she is missing out.

Itzel puts it out of her mind as she climbs a tree and begins harvesting its fruit. One by one she drops the avocados to the ground below, trying to land them in her basket. Only two hit their target. The others land nearby. Once she has picked enough to fill her basket, she clambers down the tree, gathers the avocados, and begins the short journey back toward the meager cluster of buildings that make up Cuzacal.

She stops abruptly. Puzzled, she looks toward the towers of Tikal.

Something is wrong. She knows it. Every voice and sound of merry celebration has ended in sudden silence.

Or, perhaps, she tells herself, *the wind changed and is dragging the noise elsewhere.*

Still, Itzel can't escape the dread feeling that things are not as they should be. A chill crawls down her spine, and she picks up her pace.

Reentering her grandmother's hut, Itzel places the basket on the table.

"*Mim?*" she calls, glancing around the room. Her brow is furrowed with worry.

Grandmother Xoc's chair is empty.

Itzel dashes to the bedroom curtain and pokes her head through to the other side. Except for the solitary cot on the floor, the small room is empty.

"Grandmother Xoc!" the girl cries, panic rising in her throat. "Where are you?"

There is no reply.

Tears well in her eyes. Her stomach feels sick, and her breath is tight and shallow.

Itzel is about to cry out again when she hears a whimper from somewhere outside. Tortillas and avocados forgotten, she dashes from the house and pricks up her ears, listening for the source of the sound.

The cries are coming from Aapo's hut. Itzel sprints there as fast as her legs will carry her.

When she steps inside, the first thing she sees is a jar smashed on the ground. A puddle sits among the shards, creating a muddy paste in the hut's dirt floor.

A stifled sob draws Itzel's attention to the far corner. There, with his knees pulled close to his chest, Aapo is weeping. But his cries are not those born of sorrow. They are cries of fear and shock.

"Aapo," Itzel says soothingly.

The boy glances up at her as she kneels beside him. He wipes the tears from his dirty face and tries to look braver.

"What happened, Aapo?" asks Itzel. She is afraid to hear the answer.

The boy sniffles and shakes his head, unable to find the right words. After a few deep breaths, he speaks with a trembling voice. "They ... disappeared. My mother. My sister!"

"They disappeared?" a bewildered Itzel repeats. "What do you mean?"

"One moment my mother was standing right there," Aapo explains, pointing at the broken jar in the middle of the room. "Then she disappeared. Like a spirit. Into nothing! Her jar fell to the ground and broke. I turned to shield my little sister from the shards, but she was gone too!"

Like the pottery, Aapo's brave composure shatters, and he breaks into hysterics. He seizes Itzel's arm and pulls her close, shrieking, "Where did they go, Itzel? Where are they?"

Itzel doesn't answer right away. Instead, she pulls the boy closer and makes soothing noises to calm him. Only when his sobs have sputtered and died does she finally say, "Grandmother Xoc is missing also, and I do not know where she went."

"What should we do?" moans Aapo. His eyes are bloodshot and teary and filled with hopelessness.

"We will wait here until our families return from Tikal," Itzel replies. "Maybe they will have answers."

Itzel sits next to Aapo and places a comforting arm around his shoulder. But her sick feeling is growing worse, for she remembers the sudden silencing of the city.

How long they sit without speaking, Itzel doesn't know. She becomes lost in her own imaginative fears as she wonders what has happened to everyone. Before long, the sitting and waiting grow impossible for her. The need for answers is too great in her heart.

"Come with me," she says. Realizing that Aapo has fallen asleep, she nudges him awake. "We should search Cuzacal. Perhaps there are others still here."

Aapo gives her a feeble nod, and they stand up together.

Cuzacal is a tiny village. There are only a handful of huts. It doesn't take long for Itzel and Aapo to search them all.

But they do not find a single soul.

The sun is high in its race along the sky when Itzel declares, "We must take the jungle path to Tikal. Maybe we will find my family or your father there."

Aapo seems nervous about walking the path by themselves, but he swallows the lump in his throat and nods his agreement.

Hand in hand, the two children leave the safety of the village clearing and enter beneath the shadow of the great jungle trees. The path is easy to follow. Itzel has walked it a hundred times with her parents and brother, but never alone. Never with only Aapo at her side.

The brave girl keeps her eyes moving and her mind sharp. Many dangers exist in the jungle, both animal and human. She realizes that whatever caused her grandmother and Aapo's mother and sister to vanish could now be stalking them also. The idea unsettles her, but not nearly as much as the absolute silence which has settled over Tikal. She hoped they would hear sounds of life as they drew nearer, but not even one lonely voice reaches her ears.

As they round the final curve in the jungle path, the city opens before them, confirming Itzel's worst fears.

There is no one. The streets are deserted.

"Where are they?" Aapo whispers miserably.

"Maybe we have to look for them," replies Itzel, her own voice faltering. "Maybe they gathered at the center of Tikal for—for something."

Aapo says nothing. It is clear he doesn't believe this to be the case.

The children walk deeper into the city and its silence. In the marketplaces they find booths finely displayed with foods and trinkets and pottery and other merchandise. But there is no one to sell them. In the squares where there should be dancers and music and hundreds of onlookers, there are only stray dogs taking advantage of the unguarded food.

For hours they walk up and down the streets of the city, until the sun is low over the horizon. But there is never any change.

Tikal, one of the great cities of the Mayan people, is empty.

Except for one young boy and one young girl, all its people have disappeared. And they left not a single clue where they might have gone.

Chapter Two

THE ITALIAN

"ARE YOU ALRIGHT, DEAR?"

The young man glances up from his coffee. His dark eyes dart about, broken from their trance.

A concerned woman with curly white hair is staring at him from the next table. A newspaper flutters in her wrinkled hand. The date on top reads: *FRIDAY, 25 MARCH 1938.* The main headline beneath it tells something about a break-in at the Vatican in Rome.

Nervously, the man offers the elderly woman a feeble grin and nods his assurance that he is, indeed, alright.

Even as he does, he squeezes the handle of his large suitcase. He hasn't let go of it since boarding the boat. With his free hand, he pulls a handkerchief from the front pocket of his suitcoat and uses it to sponge away the sweat on his tan forehead. He has been aboard the passenger ferry for a whole morning and has vomited twice into the emerald waters of the Tyrrhenian Sea. Still, his stomach seems unable to calm down. Neither the fresh air of the deck nor the light lunch has worked to settle his insides.

But seasickness is not the worst of his worries today.

He glances from side to side, then peeks down at his watch. He left Palermo on the island of Sicily shortly after six o'clock that morning. This means he has less than an hour until arriving at Naples on the Italian mainland. He has arranged for a car to meet him there. With any luck, he will cross the border into Switzerland—and safety— before the next sunrise.

Until then, the fresh-faced man with the slick side part in his dark hair knows he is vulnerable. His enemies are many, and they are powerful.

Ettore Majorana grips the suitcase tightly, peering into the distant horizon. Eastward, the rocky coastline of southern Italy rises from the sea like the golden teeth of some great monster. To the north, the direction his ship is heading, he recognizes the Sorrentine Peninsula. After the ship sails around this pointed spit of land, he and the rest of the passengers will arrive at the lively seaport of Naples.

Almost there, he reassures himself. *Then I will be safe. Then no one can touch me.*

But Ettore's hopeful musings do not last long.

"Excuse me," the elderly woman chirps again. She seems to be stealing quick, furtive glances at something behind Ettore. "Do you know those men? Sitting a few tables back? They have seemed quite interested in you for some time now."

His eyes grow wide, and his heart shrinks with fear.

"Are they friends of yours?" the woman inquires.

In a low whisper, Ettore asks, "What do they look like?"

The woman squints for a better look, then answers, "One tall, one fat. The fat one has a mustache, and the tall one is quite handsome. Both are wearing dark pinstripe suits."

Ettore's blood turns icy in his veins. Certainly these are the same men who approached him yesterday in Palermo's beautiful Piazza

Pretoria. Luckily for him, he had stashed the suitcase at a friend's apartment. They harassed him a bit and made some meager threats, but as long as the suitcase was safe, they were unable to cause any real damage.

Now the suitcase sits at his feet. He is uncertain whether these men will kill in order to obtain it, but he does know what resides inside the suitcase is worth one human life—perhaps more.

"Please, will you do me a favor?" Ettore pleads with the woman. "Those are bad men. They are trying to rob me of something very valuable. Already they have made many threats against my life and the lives of my family."

The old woman's eyes narrow. She plainly does not like men who rob and make threats.

"I'll help," she whispers, unable to hide her excitement.

"Good," Ettore says with a slight grin. "Take your drink and get up as if you are leaving to go belowdecks. As you pass, stumble and spill your glass over them and their table. I can use the diversion to sneak away and hide."

"But why not go to the authorities?" wonders the old woman.

"Because," Ettore answers, "these are not the sort of men whom the authorities will stop. These are the sort of men who hold authority *over* the authorities. Do you understand? Will you still help me?"

"Of course I will!" she says. She stands and smooths her black, flower-printed dress. With one hand she grabs her oversized handbag and newspaper. She picks up her wine glass with the other. Before undertaking her mission, she whispers, "Good luck," then sets off.

Moments later, Ettore hears an angry exclamation followed by the tinkling of shattered glass. As his accomplice cries her profuse apologies to the men in black suits, Ettore slips away from his table, suitcase in hand, and rounds the corner to the ferry's stern. He is out of sight here, but he cannot relax yet. The moment they see him missing, they will begin their hunt for him.

A new volley of shouts—these ones curses—erupts from around the corner. The men have realized Ettore is no longer at his table. He hears the scuffle of crashing chairs and knows what it means.

They are coming for him.

With no time to form a plan, Ettore hurries through a narrow doorway. His eyes are accustomed to the bright daylight, which is why he doesn't notice the staircase in the darkness. Like a surprised octopus, he becomes a frenzy of flailing limbs as slips and stumbles and finally collapses at the bottom of the stairs.

Ettore is certain he is covered in cuts and bruises, but he cannot dwell on the pain right now. Frantically, he sweeps the dropped suitcase back into his arms. Both its latches came undone when he fell, so he clutches it to his chest to keep it shut.

Glancing around, he sees that he is in a dimly lit corridor. There are no other passengers here.

Suddenly, the potent sunlight pouring through the doorway is obscured in shadow. Ettore instinctively looks upward and, with the frightful sensation of a cornered animal, sees the broad-bodied figure of one pursuer.

"It's over, Ettore," the fat man says calmly. "The game is up. There is nowhere for you to run anymore. Hand over the suitcase, and we can put this nasty business behind us."

The top step creaks beneath the pursuer's weight as he begins down the staircase.

Ettore dashes down the corridor. On the righthand wall, he spots a lonely doorway. The sign indicates that through it he will find the women's lavatory. He hesitates. His sense of modesty, due to his proper upbringing, makes him pause. A quick glance backward, however, reveals that both men are at the bottom of the staircase.

Ettore knows he is out of options. He slips into the lavatory and latches the door behind him. But the wood panels separating him from his pursuers are hardly thicker than cardboard. It won't take them long to beat down the door.

And, once they do, the game truly will be up.

"Come, Majorana, open this door," implores a silky voice, which Ettore recognizes as belonging to the smaller man. "A scientist like you, with such a brilliant career already in his back pocket! You don't want it all to end like this, holed up in a ladies' lavatory. This is not suitable for a man of your intellect. Your station."

He can't be certain, but he thinks he hears the drawing of a pistol hammer. He crams his body into the narrow space between the toilet and the far wall. As if his suitcase were filled with an elixir of eternal life, Ettore hugs it against his chest and waits for the worst.

There are no gunshots—not yet. Instead, the men outside pound against the door.

Ettore closes his eyes, wincing with each blow. Wood splinters. Hinges creak. The lock rattles.

He presses his face against the suitcase and prays that some deck hand or crew member might hear the commotion and apprehend them. These aren't the kind of men who will be stopped for good, but it could buy him enough time for an escape.

Suddenly, Ettore gasps and cries out.

He is falling, but he doesn't know how or why. As he opens his eyes, he sees not the dark walls of the lavatory. He sees instead the brilliant sunshine and a sky full of gray-bellied clouds. Before he can understand what has happened, his brief fall is broken.

Cold seawater envelopes him. It swirls around his legs, his torso, his head, filling his mouth and nostrils.

He resurfaces, sputtering and coughing up water.

Most importantly, Ettore realizes he is still holding the suitcase. Treading water with his legs, he hurriedly relatches the clasps which popped loose during his tumble down the stairs. He doesn't want the ancient object inside to wind up at the bottom of the ocean—as its counterpart did.

Ettore glances in every direction for the ferry. But it is gone. Not merely behind him, sailing away into the distance. The boat has disappeared entirely. A moment earlier, Ettore was cowering on a bathroom floor deep in its dark belly. Now it has vanished. Evaporated. Like liquid beneath the hot sun.

But this isn't the time to be mystified. There will be plenty of opportunity for the solving of mysteries later. Now is the time for surviving.

Ettore notes the sun in its downward arc toward the western horizon. Using it like a compass, he swims north. If he keeps in that direction, he knows he should reach the Sorrentine Peninsula before too long. The ferry, he remembers, had been approaching that landmark before his escape into the lavatory. All he needs to do is tread water—made easier with the buoyant suitcase—and propel himself forward with his legs. It will not be an enjoyable afternoon, but he should reach safety soon enough.

At least he still has his prize. He whispers a short prayer, hoping the suitcase won't become waterlogged and sink. If it does, all his trouble will have been for nothing. He remembers then that the suitcase's interior chamber is sealed, completely airtight to protect the item inside, and his confidence builds. It will not sink, and neither will he.

The sun is setting when Ettore finally arrives at the rock-studded shore. His aching legs carry his drenched body up a squat, stony hill.

The moment he reaches the grassy field on top, he collapses. Lying with his cheek pressed against the earth, he sees the scattered, squat buildings of a rustic village in the distance. It isn't far, maybe a mile.

Though every muscle in his body resists, he clambers to his feet. The heavy suitcase bounces against his left leg as he trudges wearily toward the village. He finds it strange that none of its electric lamps are glowing yet. The sun set some time ago, and twilight now covers the land.

Ettore shivers against the night's settling chill. He must find a warm room and a dry pair of clothes. Soon.

As he nears the buildings, he encounters more strange sights. The cars parked in front of them are unlike any he has ever seen, sleek and streamlined and painted with bright colors. The rooftops of some homes have gray, concave discs attached to them. They appear to be pointing upward toward the sky, as if receiving transmissions from outer space. Someone has abandoned a bicycle on the righthand side of the road. Its frame and wheels are half the size of Ettore's own bicycle, and it is emblazoned with the letters *BMX*.

Ahead of him, he sees that one of the futuristic cars has plowed into the side of a one-story home. Despite the gaping hole in the wall, no one seems to have cared enough to fix it, or even to remove the automobile. Creeping vines have grown up around both car and home, binding them together in their strange marriage.

The town, he realizes, is utterly abandoned. There isn't a light on in any window, nor a single child running around outside, enjoying the final minutes of dusk.

Wherever he is, he is surely alone.

Ettore shudders against the chill. Out of other options, he at last resorts to breaking and entering. He doesn't think anyone will mind, because there *is* no one to mind.

He chooses a single-story brick house across the street from the one eating the car.

The front door is unlocked.

Ettore steps inside and peers about the darkness. Nothing looks right. Furniture, lamps, decorations—he has never seen anything like them. A flat, black rectangle hangs on one wall, its dark screen covered in a thin film of dust. In the kitchen he finds a stove with no knobs and a completely smooth surface. The word *convection* is printed in white letters near the front. An egg-shaped appliance called an "air fryer" sits on the counter next to tiny pods claiming to hold coffee inside them.

"Where am I?" Ettore asks the dark and empty room.

The room doesn't answer.

Then the truth hits him. He sets the suitcase on the kitchen floor and collapses beside it. Following such a bizarre afternoon, the shock of discovery has turned his legs to jelly.

In wondering *where* he has come, Ettore realizes he's been asking the wrong question.

He corrects himself with a whisper. "*When* am I?"

Then, in a home not his own, and in a time not his own, Ettore Majorana slips into an exhausted sleep.

Chapter Three

SOPHIA FARADAY

THE GIRL GRITS HER TEETH, digging her fingertips into the bare rock as a powerful gust of wind punches her in the back. The breeze turns her sweaty, golden-brown hair into tiny whips which lash her freckle-brushed face. A few loose strands end up stuck in her eyes. She waits to brush them clear until the wind dies down and she can safely let go of the rock.

Sophia Faraday stares out across a world that has turned brick red. The sun is taking its last breaths before night smothers its fire. Its final embers cascade across the landscape of barren sandstone, and Arches National Park is set on fire.

It is a lifeless beauty, but beauty all the same, and the girl's eyes feast on it.

Then a dog barks far below her, and the spell is broken. Sophia tries peering down to see what has gotten Bixby so excited, but doing so makes her instantly dizzy. Her delicate position on top of Delicate Arch, the park's most famous sandstone formation, is a precarious one. She decides she had better climb down anyway before too much light has gone. Tied securely to her safety lines, she begins her descent.

"Don't worry, I'm coming down!" she reassures her dog, who still hasn't stopped his frantic barking.

There are only two reasons Bixby barks like this: when he is trying to play with some critter, or when he is worried about her. Sophia guesses that in this case, he has seen enough of her feet dangling fifty feet above solid ground and wants her safely by his side again.

"Dumb dog," she mutters, even as she grins. She knows just how devastated she would be if she ever lost her best friend. Her *only* friend.

Sophia carefully chooses both handholds and footholds. She wonders how long it has been since someone last climbed Delicate Arch. Faded signs all over the park warn visitors against scaling the landmarks here, but those rules haven't been enforced for a long time. Nowadays, she is quite certain no one will mind.

When she reaches the bottom, she unclips her safety line and brushes her hands clean of red sandstone dust. She straps her headlamp to her forehead. By its light, she gathers her climbing equipment, stuffing everything into a backpack.

"Bixby, come on!" she calls to the dog. He still hasn't stopped barking. If anything, he has grown louder and more frantic.

Sophia aims her headlamp at Bixby, seventy pounds of hyperactive boxer mutt wrapped in bristly, tawny fur. All four of his paws look like he dipped them in white paint, and a dark streak like a skid mark runs along his back. When her light finds him, he's yapping at a thick bush of purple sage pressed up against a sandstone wall.

Whatever is in there must be fascinating, Sophia thinks. Her pooch isn't usually much of a barker.

"Hey! Bixby!" she shouts again. "We have to head back now. Come on!"

The dog glances back and forth between Sophia and the bush. He whines, pleading for more time with whatever new friend he has discovered.

"Nope," she tells him firmly. "It's getting dark, and we have to walk two miles back."

After a final, longing look into the bush, Bixby obeys and follows.

The sky is an inky shade of navy and studded with stars by the time they return to the parking lot. The final remnants of sunlight will fade away within the next fifteen minutes. Sophia knows if she comes back outside then, she will witness one of her favorite sights: the brilliant arm of the Milky Way floating above her. It used to be that someone could only see the band of Earth's galaxy if they went far, far away from any cities.

Now the Milky Way is visible from anywhere—so long as the night is cloudless and clear.

There are a few other vehicles parked neatly around the lot. Sophia's motorhome, however, is parked across five spaces, and the tarp-covered trailer behind it takes up a sixth. These days she spends most of her time touring across the United States in the mammoth motorhome. She prefers bouncing between national parks and other outdoor locations. There are times, too, when she explores America's once-great urban centers, but she only goes into the cities to collect important souvenirs.

The original Declaration of Independence and the Star of India sapphire are her favorites so far. She also has the ruby slippers from *The Wizard of Oz,* her mom's favorite movie, on display in her basement, as well as a handful of Pittsburgh Steelers Superbowl rings.

Sophia opens the motorhome door, and Bixby bounds inside ahead of her. She turns on the interior lights, then drops her backpack onto the small kitchen table. After a quick glance to make sure nothing is out of place, she retreats to the bedroom and exchanges her climbing clothes for pajama pants, fuzzy socks, and a long-sleeved tee depicting characters from *The Lion King.*

When she steps into the tiny bathroom to wash up, Bixby starts barking again. She ignores him, thinking he must be caught in a weird mood.

As she rinses her calloused hands under the warm water, she notices the deep scars that she hates so much. Like an ugly, permanent bracelet, they wrap all the way around her left wrist.

Shackled to those scars is a memory so painful, she would give anything to forget it. Yet she knows it is one she will remember for the rest of her life.

Sophia looks away from the scars and stares into the small mirror above the sink. Every time she does, she realizes anew how much she has changed. Her hazel eyes, once bright and cheery, look hard and tired. While her hair has always been the color of golden caramel, these days it also feels sticky like caramel, and is often coated with grease and grime. She almost always sports it in a ponytail to keep it away from her face and neck. Although she has been thin her whole life, the last couple years have turned her into a leaner, more muscular version of herself. Her cheekbones and jawline are certainly not those of a young girl. They must belong to someone in her twenties or thirties—not a twelve-year-old kid like her.

For the thousandth time, Sophia can't help but feel that she has been cheated out of her childhood. No one should have to experience what she has.

As soon as the thoughts start creeping in, Sophia closes her eyes. She takes a deep breath and pushes back against the bitterness. She has taken too many journeys down that road in the past two and a half years. Silently, she renews the promise she made to herself. She will never wander into that darkness again. Too much has been stolen already. She can't steal even more from herself by living a bitter and resentful life.

Bixby is still barking, she realizes with a fluttering sense of alarm. Whatever has gotten into him, it doesn't seem to be going away anytime soon.

"What's wrong, buddy?" she asks. She pokes her head into the motorhome's main cabin, which houses the kitchen, dining area, and living room.

The dog gives her a sideways glance. He whines, as if adding an exclamation mark to his outburst, then returns to his barking.

Thinking he might be acting out of hunger—it *is* almost ten o'clock—she fills his bowls with food and water.

He isn't interested.

"Whatever, Bix," she mutters, opening a cupboard stocked with dozens of cans. "Bark all you want."

Sophia selects a can of cheesy ravioli with an easy-open, pull-top tab. She empties the saucy morsels into a bowl and places it in the microwave. Three minutes later, she's sitting at the narrow table, enjoying her dinner.

Bixby, who usually sits next to the table begging for scraps, still hasn't quieted down. The only change is that he's no longer barking at the front door. He is now on Sophia's bed, barking at the back window.

The noise is giving her a headache, but it's the dog's insistent behavior she finds far more distressing.

She leaves her half-eaten dinner on the table and makes her way to the front of the vehicle. She's tempted to drive away but remembers that the motorhome isn't roadworthy yet. The tarp and straps are all loose on the trailer. Plus, she needs to secure the awning, which is currently propped up outside the front door.

Instead of jumping into the driver's chair, she clambers into the passenger seat. When she opens the glovebox, its faint yellow light illuminates a ten-inch-long, silvery steel object.

The pistol. She hates it, yet won't travel without it.

Not after the Asheville incident.

She shudders to think about it. She can still smell the moldy odor of the foul house, feel the ropes around her hands and feet, hear the crazy cackles from her basement prison.

Never again. She will never be caught off guard like that again.

Pistol in hand, Sophia returns to the dining area. Bixby is now running back and forth and spinning in circles. He is more frenzied, more frantic than before. Fierce growls accompany his shrill yelps, and every hair on his back stands on end.

"Bixby!" she hisses. "Shut *up!*"

To her surprise, he obeys. He trots to the front door and faces her expectantly, certain she will finally let him out.

Sophia does. Gripping the pistol in her right hand, she flings the door open. Bixby is a flurry of paws and fur as he tumbles through it and onto the gravel. Outside, he performs an immediate U-turn, raising his eyes and snout toward the dark sky.

Whatever he's barking at, it's on the motorhome's roof.

A lump like a stone catches in Sophia's throat. She swipes the headlamp from the hook next to the door, slides its elastic band around her head, and turns it on. After swallowing a deep breath, she hurls herself outside. Skidding to a halt next to Bixby, she pivots, aiming both headlamp and pistol toward the roof.

Her mind is in overdrive, running at the speed of light. She has no idea what to expect. A mountain lion? A bear? Something worse?

Her finger tightens on the trigger.

"Who's there?" Sophia calls into the darkness. Her voice trembles like a teenager asking someone out on a first date—not that *she'd* know. Trying to summon her confidence and courage, she adds, "Show yourself right now! *Right now!*"

Nothing happens, other than Bixby's strange decision to spin in a tight circle.

Sophia aims a harmless, sideways kick at him. Through gritted teeth she growls, "Bixby. Shut. Up." The stress on each individual word does the trick, and the dog falls silent.

Her trembling hands keep the pistol pointed upward as she shuffles toward the back of the motorhome. Her heart is beating like a drum at a rock concert. Moving her tongue around her mouth, she tries to work some moisture into it, but jittery nerves have left it bone dry. She fears something may also be lurking in the darkness behind her, but Bixby's attention remains fixed on the roof, so she figures hers should be too.

Sophia freezes. Her eyes go wide, and her heart vaults into her throat.

Something moved, melting back into the darkness the moment her light fell on it.

She tries to speak, but her voice falters. Mustering every shred of courage she has left, she tries again.

"I—I saw you!" Sophia stutters. "Stop hiding! Come into the light with your hands up. If you don't, I'm gonna start shooting. And I promise, I'm an excellent shot."

She prays her bluff pays off. The truth is, she's only shot the pistol three times. Occasionally she has gone hunting, but she has always used a bow. And in a world where most animals have lost their fear of humans, they're usually standing still.

Much easier targets than a desperate—possibly crazed—human being.

The old woman's face resurfaces in Sophia's mind. She sees the filthy, tangled hair. The sick, wicked smile missing half its yellowed teeth. The wild, bloodshot eyes.

For one tiny moment, Sophia is certain *she* will emerge into the light. Certain that *she* has come to finish what she started so long ago.

But that would be impossible. Sophia knows it. Like a human Etch-a-Sketch, she shakes her head and clears the woman's image from her mind's eye.

"Listen," Sophia calls out, "I'm going to count to three. If you don't come out with your hands up by then, I *will* shoot! Got it?"

No answer.

"One!"

Her finger tightens on the trigger.

"Two!"

"Okay! Okay!" a shaky voice cries out. It is more high-pitched than Sophia would have imagined.

The speaker—whoever it is—sounds scared.

But Sophia isn't ready to back down. She yells, "Come into the light! Now!"

She hears shuffling on top of the motorhome. Two beat-up sneakers step cautiously into the headlamp's beam.

Sophia tilts her head back a few degrees to reveal the rest of the nighttime intruder.

Her jaw drops.

Standing there, hands raised high, trembling and wide-eyed with terror, is a young boy no older than nine.

Some hidden dam bursts in Sophia's heart, and tears well in her eyes.

He's the first person she has seen in two whole years.

Chapter Four

A CONVERSATION WITH COCOA

SOPHIA LOWERS THE PISTOL at once. She steps forward and stretches her gun-free hand toward the frightened boy.

"Come down," she croaks, her voice hoarse and relieved. "Don't be scared. I won't hurt you. Please, come down."

The boy stares back. He squints against the light, but other than this, his expression remains blank.

Sophia notices how thin he is, and wonders when he last enjoyed a decent meal. His red hair is long and stringy, and the plentiful freckles on his dirt-streaked face look like a human connect-the-dots. His *Jurassic Park* t-shirt, on the other hand, appears almost new, as do his blue jeans.

She also notices that he is shivering. At first, she thought he was trembling with fear. Now she realizes his chattering teeth tell the tale of a boy outside too long on a chilly night.

"Come inside and warm up," she urges. "Please. You're freezing. There's a ladder in back. You can use that."

The boy moves warily toward the motorhome's rear, where a narrow ladder joins bumper to roof. Aided by the light of Sophia's headlamp, he climbs down until his shoes land with a *crunch* upon the gravel.

Bixby, always the friendly dog, approaches the boy. His tail whips vigorously back and forth. Now that he sees Sophia relaxing, his worries about the intruder have vanished.

But the boy's worries remain. He steps backward, away from the dog.

"It's okay," Sophia assures him. "He's very nice. He just didn't know who you were before. He probably thought you were a bad guy. Hold out your hand and let him smell you."

The boy hesitates, then does as told.

With his nose only an inch from the boy's hand, Bixby takes a few good whiffs. Then his long, pink tongue licks the dirty fingers.

Sophia notices the faintest glimmer of a grin on the boy's lips, and it brings a smile to her own.

"So, will you come in?" she asks again.

He nods.

Five minutes later, he's sitting at the motorhome's little table. Bixby is next to him, resting his head the boy's lap. Fear and mistrust forgotten, he scratches the dog gently behind the ears. In front of him is a steaming mug of cocoa beside a bowl he has licked clean of every trace of cheesy ravioli.

Sophia, who gave the rest of her dinner to him, removes a second bowl from the microwave to replace the empty one. Apparently unaffected by the scalding heat, the boy begins wolfing it down immediately.

"You should probably chew it a little," Sophia says. She finds his starved eating both amusing and a bit sad at the same time. "You're gonna get an upset stomach if you don't."

The boy glances up at her timidly, as if afraid he might offend her, and slows his pace. Tomato sauce dribbles down his chin as he eats, but he doesn't seem to notice or care. When he is finished with the food, he grabs the cocoa mug and downs half of it. After wiping his mouth with the back of his hand, he sets the mug on the table and looks at Sophia with dark, bleary eyes.

"Thanks," he mutters.

It's the first word he has spoken since coming down from the roof.

"You're welcome," Sophia replies warmly.

"What's your name?" he asks meekly. He still seems worried he might upset his hostess. And her gun.

"I'm Sophia," she answers. "Sophia Faraday. Who're you?"

"Gabriel," he replies.

Sophia scuffs the floor nervously with her toe. She is surprised to find herself at a loss for words. On lonely nights, she has often spoken to her mom and dad as if they were really with her. When watching a beautiful sunset, she has described it aloud to her missing brothers, who would have loved to see it. But now she realizes just how long it has been since she had a real conversation with another person.

It isn't as easy as she remembers.

"You were up by the arch tonight, weren't you?" she asks, although she already knows the answer.

The boy—Gabriel—nods.

"That's what was making Bixby go so crazy," continues Sophia. "You were scared, so you hid in the bush!"

Gabriel nods again but doesn't say anything. He finishes his cocoa in three gulps, then eyes Sophia hopefully.

"Do you want more?" she asks.

Again, he nods but doesn't speak.

"I'll get you some, but only if you start talking!" she tells him, trying to sound as warm as possible. She wants him to feel comfortable but realizes this might be difficult. Fifteen minutes ago, she *was* pointing a gun at him.

"Now," she says, when there is a second mug of cocoa in front of him, "will you tell me how you found me?"

Gabriel nods. He seems to be choosing his words carefully.

That's when it strikes Sophia—little Gabriel also hasn't had a conversation in a very long time. Words might be tougher for him to come by.

Eventually, he says, "I'm from Grand Junction. In Colorado. That's how I found you. I climbed on the roof when you stopped to put gas in your car." When he says the word *car*, he indicates the whole motorhome. He isn't sure what to call it.

Sophia thinks back and remembers Bixby going crazy with the barking then too. At the time, she figured he was feeling cooped up after their long drive. Really it was because a little hitchhiker was hitching his ride to Utah on their roof.

Her mouth drops in astonishment, and she says, "You mean you were hanging on that whole time? For two hours?"

Gabriel shrugs. His eyes are downcast, and his voice cracks as he whispers, "I didn't want to be alone anymore."

Sophia feels her own emotions rising into her chest and throat. How many nights did she herself spend soaking her pillow in tears? How many days was she too sad even to eat anything? She remembers a loneliness so heavy, she sometimes thought she would die from it. And she's had Bixby with her the whole time! She wonders how much sadder, and lonelier, and more difficult life has been for this boy named Gabriel since—

Since everyone disappeared.

"Well, you aren't alone anymore," she says with a kind smile. "You can stay with us." She glances down at her dog, whose head is still resting on Gabriel's lap, and adds, "Besides, I think Bixby likes you too much to let you go."

Gabriel grins and scratches the soft fur behind the dog's floppy ears. He asks, "Can we go back to my house so I can get my things? I know it's a long way back, but—"

Sophia cuts him off. "Yes, for sure we can! My house—well, I guess it's more like my home base—is near Denver. Do you know where that is?"

Gabriel nods and says, "I was there a few times with my family when I was little."

"Anyway," continues Sophia, "we can stop and get your stuff on our way back to Denver."

After a short silence, Gabriel asks, "How old are you?"

"I'm twelve," Sophia answers. Things like time and age don't seem to matter anymore, but she has kept track of every single day since being on her own. And, as lame as it must seem, she has also done something special on her birthday each year. "How 'bout you?" she asks.

"Nine, I think," Gabriel says uncertainly. "It was my sixth birthday when everyone disappeared. I was outside playing in the snow with my mom and my sisters. We were almost going back inside, and then they were ... *gone*. I ran around everywhere looking for them and couldn't find them. Then I tried calling 9-1-1, but no one answered. And then I heard a car crash into the neighbor's house next door, so I went over there, but there was no one in the car, and Mr. Pitts, who *never* left home, wasn't there either."

Sophia watches the pain grow in Gabriel's face as he relives the terror of his story. She wants him to stop for his own sake, but he keeps going. Now that he is finally talking, the years of bottled-up words keep gushing.

"I tried knocking on every neighbor's house on my street, but there was no one," he says. "I heard a bunch of crashes, and there was so much smoke, and I even saw a plane crash in the middle of town. But I never saw any people. And my dad never came home that night. I fell asleep, and when I woke up, everything was quiet. I walked around all day. I looked for people in all the houses and the grocery store. But everyone was disappeared."

Gabriel's tears leave streaks down his filthy cheeks as he whimpers, "You're the first person I've seen since then. I thought I was the last person alive *anywhere.*"

Sophia doesn't know what to say. So much about Gabriel's story is similar to her own. All alone. Fending for himself. Scratching out a survival. Yet she cannot help but notice that some of the key details are very different.

"So you were actually *here* when everyone disappeared?" she asks him curiously.

Gabriel nods, confused by her simple question.

"I ... wasn't," Sophia says.

The boy's eyes widen with surprise. "You weren't? But then, how can you be here?"

Sophia chuckles and answers, "I don't really know. It's a mystery to me too. I don't know *how* any of this happened. I can only tell you *what* happened."

But a quick glance at the clock, and then at Gabriel's drooping eyes, reminds her how late it is, so she says, "Maybe that's a story for tomorrow. I can tell you about it when we're on the road. Right now, I think we both need some sleep."

Gabriel frowns but doesn't protest.

"You can have my bed in back," offers Sophia. "It's super comfy. Lots of pillows and blankets. I'll sleep on the couch out here."

"Are you sure?" Gabriel asks hesitantly.

"Yeah, I'm sure. But just for tonight! When we get back to Denver, we'll figure out something else. Maybe we can find a motorhome with *two* beds!"

Sophia leads Gabriel to the small bedroom in back, and he flops down on the soft mattress.

"I have an extra toothbrush somewhere," she says. "You should brush your teeth, especially after drinking all that cocoa."

She suddenly realizes how much she sounds like her mom. Maria Faraday had been a dentist. She was *always* worried about sugary drinks.

"Okay," mumbles Gabriel, whose voice is muffled by the blankets pressed against his face.

Sophia didn't plan on becoming a mother when she woke up that morning. Now here she is, rummaging through the bathroom cabinet for an extra toothbrush. During the last hour, she has gone from a two-year loneliness to taking care of a nine-year-old boy. That morning her to-do list for the next few weeks included visiting a half-dozen national parks. Tomorrow's list now has her returning to Gabriel's home in Grand Junction for more *Jurassic Park* shirts—or whatever it is he's planning to pick up there.

But it's worth it. It's worth changing every plan she made. Because now she won't be alone anymore.

Sophia chooses a green toothbrush from the toiletry box in the cabinet and returns to the bedroom.

"Here's your—" she starts to say, but she stops mid-sentence.

Gabriel is fast asleep and snoring lightly.

Sophia turns out the lights. She leaves the door open a crack in case Bixby wants to lie on the mattress next to him, then puts the toothbrush on a little shelf in the bathroom. As quietly as she can, she brushes her own teeth, turns out the rest of the lights, and collapses onto the sofa. She pulls a heavy, denim quilt up to her chin, the one her mom made when she was pregnant with Sophia. She likes to imagine that it still smells like her long-gone family.

She closes her eyes but doesn't fall asleep. Her mind and her heart are too full.

Annoyed by her restlessness, Bixby eventually slinks into the bedroom to sleep beside Gabriel.

Any other night she would have forced the dog to stay with her. But not tonight. Tonight, she doesn't mind.

Because, for the first time in a long time, Sophia Faraday does not feel alone.

Chapter Five

THE WESTBOUND TRAIN

SOPHIA AWAKENS TO A BRONZE glow. The morning sunlight is forcing its way through the motorhome's beige curtains. She rolls over to check the time on the microwave clock and almost jumps out of her pajamas.

Eleven o'clock came and went twenty minutes ago. She scolds herself for sleeping in so late.

Little Gabriel is still out cold. Bixby is on the bed but awake, keeping watch over his new friend.

Sophia debates whether she ought to let him sleep a little longer. Perhaps she and Bixby can hike to one of the nearby sandstone formations. But when she considers how frightened Gabriel might be to wake up and find himself alone, she abandons the idea and decides to make breakfast instead.

A steaming pile of scrambled eggs is waiting for Gabriel when he stumbles from the bedroom ten minutes later. He rubs his eyes and plunks himself down at the table.

"How do you have eggs?" the boy asks. He is amazed to find that Sophia, three years into the end of the world, has food that lasts only a few weeks before going bad.

"I raise chickens back in Denver," she replies. "I stock up every time I go home."

Gabriel's mouth is already full of breakfast. Between chews, he says, "I haven't ... had eggs ... since before everyone ... disappeared."

"We can gather more when we go back," she promises, before digging into the pile on her own plate.

Once breakfast is finished, Sophia shows Gabriel how to use the shower. She hands him a fresh, powder-blue shirt to wear, then leaves him alone to clean away the grease and grime of countless days—maybe years. When he emerges a while later, he looks like a brand-new boy. His red hair is bright and bouncy, and his freckles appear more pronounced without a layer of dirt smeared over them. Even his eyes are clearer and more alive than last night.

Sophia showers too, then turns her attention to readying the motorhome for travel. She secures her spare gas cans—always a good idea to carry plenty extra—onto the trailer behind the motorhome, tying them down with bungee cords and rope. Once she has double-checked the trailer hitch, she stows the awning and gauges the air pressure in the tires.

"All set!" she announces to Gabriel, who has been watching her work. "Ready to go?"

With a smile wider than the Grand Canyon, he nods vigorously.

Sophia calls to Bixby, who has been sniffing around one of the abandoned cars in the lot. He comes running and jumps into the motorhome, his tail wagging excitedly.

"He loves taking trips," Sophia informs Gabriel, before adding, "although he might not be too happy that you're taking the front seat from him!"

Ten minutes later, Bixby has proven that two can sit shotgun, as he lies happily across Gabriel's lap and stares out the open window at the passing scenery. The breeze crosses from Sophia to Gabriel, cool and refreshing and promising a newer, happier adventure for both.

They wind through the park's sandstone landscape before turning north onto a cracked and weed-choked highway. Here and there along the route, they see cars and semi-trucks which, suddenly driverless, plowed off the road. Other vehicles simply stopped and stalled in the middle of the highway, as if some giant toddler forgot to clean up his oversized Matchbox cars.

The obstacles force Sophia to drive with caution. The last thing she wants is to break down so far from any city. Replacement motor-homes aren't easy to come by in these remote parts.

"How did you learn to drive?" Gabriel asks, breaking a pleasant silence.

Sophia shrugs and answers, "Just had to teach myself, since no one else was around."

"I'm too short to reach any of the pedals," says Gabriel. "I tried once and crashed Mom's car right through the garage door."

"Well, I'm actually cheating," admits Sophia with a sly grin. "You can see for yourself when we stop. I have fat pieces of foam attached to the top of the pedals so I can reach 'em better."

The boy grunts and mutters, "I wish I thought of that. Maybe I could've left Grand Junction."

"I can teach you lots of the tricks I've learned: how to get more gas, how to hook up a generator to run electricity in the house, how to get fresh water from a well—tons of good stuff!"

"Did you ever see anyone else besides me?"

Gabriel's out-of-the-blue question takes Sophia by surprise. As if drawn by a powerful magnet, her mind is pulled back to Asheville. Even the earliest days alone in the new world did not hold the fear, the despair, the hopelessness she felt during her two-day captivity. Just thinking about those hours twists her gut into knots.

Eleanor. That was the old woman's name.

Was. Not anymore. Dead people, she knows, don't use their names any longer.

"Yes," she finally answers. She wanted to lie, to let the memory stay buried with the dead woman in her basement. For some reason, though, it feels wrong to hide the truth.

"Really?" Gabriel asks excitedly. "Who?"

"It doesn't matter," Sophia says softly. "She's gone. For good."

Gabriel reads her tone and changes the subject. "Why did you come out here anyway? If you live in Denver?"

"Well," responds Sophia, happy to discuss this new question, "it's because I like exploring. I've traveled all over the country. Denver is where I go when I need to relax or restock my supplies."

"Where else have you been?" he asks.

Sophia stifles a laugh. When she first met him last night, he spoke so little she wondered if he had forgotten how. Today he is a typical nine-year-old boy who can't stop asking questions.

"New York City, D.C., Boston. All over the Appalachian Mountains. You know where those are?"

Gabriel nods and says, "I think we went there when I was little. I remember staying at a cabin, and there were lots of fireflies around."

"Sounds nice," Sophia tells him, as she weaves the motorhome around a pickup truck occupying the middle of the road. "Anyway, we can go wherever you want! I've got lots of books at home about cool places to travel. You can look through them and pick out a few you think look neat."

"Really?" Gabriel looks as thrilled as the kids in the old Disney World commercials. "That'll be so awesome!"

"Definitely! It'll be fun!" she promises. She bubbles with excitement at the thought of sharing her adventures with another person, even if that other person is a little boy. "Bixby has been a good traveling buddy, but I have a feeling you'll be even better!"

Gabriel doesn't respond. When Sophia peeks over at him, she sees him staring out the window. A cheerful grin is plastered from one side of his freckled face to the other.

Two quiet minutes later, the highway exits the winding canyon and enters a flat, parched expanse of land. Like the edge of a jagged knife, mountain peaks rise upon every horizon. In these level plains between the mountains, Sophia can see for miles, and that means a quicker traveling pace. Long before reaching them, she can pinpoint and avoid vehicles—or other obstacles—in the roadway.

Sophia spots an overpass not far ahead. This is where the highway meets up with the interstate. In following this eastward, they will find themselves in Grand Junction and, eventually, back in Denver.

"How did you get here?" Gabriel asks, as Sophia begins slowing for her turn onto the onramp.

Sophia is puzzled by the question. "With the motorhome."

"No!" Gabriel exclaims. "That's not what I meant. I mean—um—how did you get *here*? Last night you said you weren't around when everyone disappeared. So how can you be here now?"

Sophia cranks the steering wheel as she says, "It's hard to explain. I don't exactly understand it myself. It's almost like I slipped forward through—"

But Sophia never finishes the thought. Like a reflex, her foot hits the brake when she glances sideways out her window. The squeal of tires is followed closely by the odor of burnt rubber, and the whole motorhome shudders as it screeches to a halt.

"What is it?" cries Gabriel. He is full of the same fear he showed the night before. "Is something wrong? Are we in trouble?"

His words are like distant echoes in Sophia's ears, and her jaw hangs limp with disbelief. She squints, certain her eyes are playing tricks on her. What she has spotted is not only insane. It's impossible.

"Sophiaaa?" Gabriel whines. He sounds like he's about to freak out completely.

She points north out her window and asks, "Do you see anything?"

Gabriel pushes Bixby off his lap. He unbuckles his seatbelt and leans over Sophia for a better look. His light-blue eyes flit back and forth, scanning the landscape for anything unusual.

For a moment his expression remains the same. Then his eyes go wide.

"Is that a *train?*" he marvels, speaking with a dramatic whisper.

"I ... think so?" replies Sophia, unable to trust what she is seeing.

A mile away, a thin cloud of oily, black smoke hangs in the air. Beneath it, a train is speeding westward, the opposite direction they are traveling. It isn't like the mile-long trains Sophia used to see at the railroad crossing by her house in Pennsylvania. This train is only three cars long. There's an engine in front, a passenger car in the middle, and a second engine facing backward.

"Do you know what this means?" Gabriel cries. "There are more people besides us! We aren't the only ones!"

The tightness returns to Sophia's chest and throat. Certainly there are people onboard the train. Any idiot would know that. But what *kind* of people are they? In her imagination, she sees a train full of Eleanors, old women like the one she killed and escaped from in Asheville. A train full of twisted minds who would imprison her— and Gabriel—for no reason whatsoever.

It was just her, she reasons with herself. *It was just one time. Not everyone can be like that. No one else can be like that! You have a chance to find friends again. A family again. Don't give that up because of one horrible person.*

"What should we do?" Gabriel asks, tearing her away from her inner thoughts.

Sophia realizes then that she isn't deciding for herself alone. She must also consider Gabriel.

And she knows they both need more.

"We're going to follow them," she announces. "We'll follow them and spy on them. Then, when we know they're safe, we'll talk to them."

Gabriel whoops his excitement.

"But," Sophia adds, "it means we won't be able get your stuff in Grand Junction. Not yet, at least. You okay with that?"

"Yes! Yes!"

Ahead is a place to make a U-turn onto the westbound side of the interstate. Sophia wheels them around, and in moments they are traveling the same direction as the train.

The change of circumstances is almost too improbable to believe. First Gabriel, and now this? Yet here she finds herself, with a human passenger sitting shotgun as they chase down even more. It is, at the same time, both exhilarating and frightening.

Late into the afternoon, they follow the train. There is one tense hour when they lose track of it in the hills of Fishlake National Forest, but after a short stop to pour more gas into the motorhome's tank, the black smoke reemerges southwest of them, and Sophia again gives chase. Soon, they see signs along the road for St. George, Utah.

Sophia knows that beyond St. George lies the empty husk of Las Vegas. She prays the train will not go any further than Sin City—as it used to be called. The sun is dipping close to the horizon, and she doesn't know whether she can follow in the dark.

All the while, Gabriel daydreams out loud about what kinds of people may be onboard. Will there be boys and girls his age? Will there be moms and dads and families? He also wonders—and it breaks Sophia's heart to hear it—whether his own family could be among the mysterious passengers.

All Sophia thinks about is where her weapons are hidden.

They pass the turnoff for Zion National Park and stop for another fill-up north of St. George. Dusk has fallen, and the train is now so far from the road that they can only see it with binoculars. Fortunately, whoever is driving the train has turned on its lights, otherwise finding it would be almost impossible.

Twilight has already swallowed the land, and Gabriel is asleep in the passenger seat, when Sophia notices the train slowing down. She taps the brakes, and the motorhome does the same. Soon, both have come to a complete stop. The train's lights darken, and Sophia also extinguishes those of her motorhome.

She slides from her seat and tiptoes to the vehicle's rear, where she grabs a pair of blankets and pillows. After beckoning Bixby out of Gabriel's lap, she throws a blanket over the boy and props a pillow beneath his head. Then she settles back into the driver's seat and curls up around her own pillow.

She doesn't plan to sleep. She plans to stay awake all night, in case the train starts moving again.

But the day has been long. Beneath the warmth of her cozy blanket, Sophia soon gives in to darkness and dreams.

Chapter Six

THE GLASS PYRAMID

SOPHIA STIRS IN HER SEAT. When her hazy mind remembers where she is and what she's doing, her eyes pop open. Daylight is filling the motorhome's cab. With a sinking feeling in her chest, she clambers out of her chair and leans over Gabriel to look out his window.

The train is gone.

"No no no no! *No!*" she hisses through gritted teeth.

Gabriel's fluttering eyelids resist waking, but he comes fully to his senses when Sophia fires up the engine.

"What's going on?" he asks with a yawn.

"The train already left," Sophia growls. She is frustrated with herself for falling asleep and letting their quarry escape. "You keep a lookout for the it. I'll keep my eyes on the road."

Bixby has been sleeping on the bed in back. Now he plants himself between the two humans. Gabriel satisfies the dog's need for attention by absentmindedly scratching him between the ears.

Sophia feels sick. They both had a chance to find more people, to be part of a community again. If they lose that opportunity because of her—if *Gabriel* loses that opportunity because of her—she will never forgive herself.

She doesn't realize how fast she's driving until Gabriel cries out with a touch of terror, "Slow down!"

Sophia reluctantly taps the brakes. Still, she speeds along much faster than she normally would.

They have a train to catch.

She glances down at the gas gauge. The motorhome only has a quarter tank left. They will have no choice but to stop within the next hour.

Silently, Sophia curses herself for not taking five minutes to fill the tank when they stopped last night. She prays that those on the train aren't planning to travel much farther.

Fifteen minutes later, Gabriel raises a long-nailed finger. Pointing ahead, he shouts, "There! I think I see it!"

Sure enough, thin wisps of smoke rise on the horizon. Before long, the train's rear is in sight.

Sophia slows down. She doesn't want to come too close. They'll make their presence known to those onboard after they have investigated and are sure such people are safe. For the moment, she prefers to remain out of sight.

They drive on. Not far down the road, there comes into view the dead and dried husk of a metropolis that was once bursting with life. The brilliant desert sun glints off the glass of abandoned casinos and high-rise office buildings, causing the city to sparkle as if Tinkerbell herself sprinkled fairy dust over it.

"What is that?" Gabriel asks, mystified.

"That," answers Sophia, "is Las Vegas."

Las Vegas, Nevada, was once known as a city where people could go wild with gambling and partying. Now it looks like a haunt for wild desert animals reclaiming what they lost to humans a hundred years earlier. The skyscrapers and casinos stand tall and proud, the gravestones of humanity at its best—and its worst.

Sophia wonders why the people on the train would want to come here. Certainly plenty of money is hidden in the city's hundreds of casinos, but in this new world, dollars and cents won't get a person very far. Nor is Las Vegas, smack dab in the middle of a desert, the kind of place where life can flourish anew. Another two hundred miles of withered earth and mountains lie beyond the city. If they were to keep driving past these thirsty lands, they would find themselves among the groves and croplands of California, a land where grapes, nuts, oranges, avocados, and all kinds of food grow in abundance.

Undoubtedly, that must be where the train is heading.

As they move closer to Vegas's downtown area, the buildings become packed tightly together. Sophia and Gabriel can see the humongous casinos clearly. One looks like a giant needle, sticking up out of the desert and topped with a UFO. A bit further away, a great pyramid of glass slices upward into the cloudless, crystal-blue sky. A thousand points of reflected sunlight give it the appearance of a gemstone cut for a giant.

The deeper they drive into the city, the more Sophia must slow the motorhome. Vacant vehicles are strewn carelessly about the road, and Sophia weaves around them cautiously. She is so focused on the road, she fails to notice what Gabriel sees.

"I think the train is slowing down," he informs her. A minute later he says, "Yep. It's *definitely* slowing down."

Sophia divides her attention between the road and the train. She is careful to stay close without alerting the people onboard to their presence.

At last, the train stops in front of a highway overpass. So does the motorhome. On the other side of the interstate are two casinos— Caesar's Palace and the Bellagio. Sophia remembers the second one from a heist movie she once watched with her parents.

Peeking over the dashboard, the two children wait for something to happen.

Five minutes pass, but nothing does.

Was it somehow a rogue train? Did they drive all this way for nothing? Could some freak occurrence have caused it to start moving on its own?

Sophia doesn't think so. The fact that it stopped for the night alleviates her doubts. That would happen only if people were operating it.

Perhaps those onboard noticed the motorhome following them. Perhaps they are purposely hiding. Perhaps they are even preparing to fight.

The girl closes her eyes, takes a deep breath, and forces herself to control her imagination. Inventing wild scenarios won't help her focus. It will only make her jumpy and cause her to make dumb, impulsive decisions. She must be a chess master, a professional athlete, a martial arts expert. Concentrated, calculated, and in a sharp state of mind.

After another minute, Sophia decides she can't wait anymore.

"Stay here with Bixby," she orders Gabriel. "I'll check it out."

Gabriel looks like she just told him to pick up a rattlesnake. "Don't leave me here!" he cries out sharply. "I want to come with."

Sophia is about to invent an excuse when she spots movement at the train.

"Freeze!" she whispers, ducking low behind the dashboard.

The door of the train's passenger compartment has slid open.

Someone steps out.

The slender black woman examines her surroundings for a few seconds, then beckons to an unseen person inside the train. A second woman, who Sophia thinks could be the twin of the first, joins her. They engage in a brief conversation before reentering the train compartment.

"What're they doing?" asks Gabriel.

Sophia realizes then how much the boy already looks up to her. Just like a child with his mother, he expects her to have answers she can't possibly know.

"Not sure," she replies. "Let's wait and see what happens."

Two more minutes crawl by.

"Maybe they saw us," Gabriel whispers. "Maybe they're going to leave again."

No sooner is the last word out of his mouth than the two women reappear. This time they're followed by another pair, both of whom look like men. One is young and fit, with wavy blonde hair curling out from beneath a black cowboy hat. The other is short and dark featured. He wears a charcoal, pinstripe suit, strange attire in a world where there's no one to impress.

It is this second man who seems to be in charge. Sophia sees him speaking to the others as he points toward the towering buildings across the interstate.

"Get your shoes on," she instructs Gabriel. "As soon as they start moving—if they move—we've gotta be ready to follow them."

Gabriel obeys wordlessly as Sophia climbs out of her seat. She retreats to the bedroom and opens the top dresser drawer. Stuffed in the corner is a leather holster, designed to be worn behind her hip and inside the waistband of her jeans. Here she can keep the pistol safely hidden until she needs to use it—*if* she needs to use it. Quickly, she straps the holster to her belt and tucks it inside her jeans, then returns to the cab.

"They're leaving!" Gabriel worriedly exclaims.

"Good," Sophia responds. She leans over him, opens the glove box, and withdraws the pistol.

Gabriel's face turns white when he sees it.

Sophia notices his reaction. "Don't worry," she assures him. "I'll only use it if I absolutely have to. Now, let's go!"

Bixby groans his disapproval when Sophia commands him to stay. Affectionately, she scratches his wrinkly forehead, then closes the door to drown out his anxious whines.

It's only midmorning, but the Las Vegas air is already hot and dry. Sophia feels like they've stepped into an oven turned to its *LOW* setting. She wishes she would have thought to fill a few water bottles, but if she does so now, they might lose sight of the train people.

They keep their distance as they follow. Sophia is careful to keep them hidden, edging along walls, sprinting between cars, and moving within shadows whenever possible.

Gabriel mimics her movements, mirroring the older girl exactly.

The two children tail the four strangers for what seems like forever in the desert heat. A pair of stealth soldiers, they creep down Las Vegas Boulevard behind the unsuspecting quartet, until they are deep within the mighty claws of the deserted casino city. They pass the dried-up pool in front of the Bellagio and the half-sized Eiffel Tower in front of Paris Las Vegas.

A sideways glimpse at Gabriel convinces Sophia they cannot continue much longer. His endurance is melting beneath the rising temperatures, and the desert furnace will only grow hotter as the day grows older. She scolds herself for leaving without water.

Ahead of them stands the black, glass-wrapped pyramid they saw from the highway. With its human head and outstretched lion's paws, a full-size replica of the ancient Egyptian Sphinx guards the entrance. In front of the stone beast is a tall, thin, pointed obelisk. Large, vertical letters spell out the word *Luxor*.

This is where the group led by the man in the suit finally veers away from the boulevard. They make for the space between the Sphinx's elephant-sized paws.

Sophia and Gabriel remain crouched behind an overturned sedan. They watch until the four are out of sight, then sprint toward the closest Sphinx paw. Sophia peeks around the corner toward the entrance doors. The strangers—whoever they are—have gone inside.

"The coast is clear," she whispers, "but I can't see past the doors. I'll go first and check it out. Wait here until I tell you to follow."

Gabriel yanks on her sleeve. The beginnings of tears are forming in his blue eyes.

"What if you don't come back?" he says. "What if they catch you?"

"They won't," says Sophia, patting the pistol hidden under her shirt and jeans. "But if they do, you run back to the motorhome and hide there. Bixby will keep you safe."

The boy is uncomforted by her words, but he lets her go anyway.

Sophia sticks close to the wall as she dashes to the front doors. Then she takes a deep breath, yanks one open, and slips inside the glass pyramid.

Chapter Seven

MAPPA MUNDI

SOPHIA'S ENTRANCE INTO the Luxor is less dramatic than expected.

Inside the first bank of glass doors, there is second set. Unlike the exterior ones, she can see through these quite easily. Beyond them is a large, open lobby. Sitting atop the opposite wall are two stone pharaohs, the rulers of ancient Egypt, keeping watch over the entrance. Between them is a wide, rectangular opening, like the mouth of a sleeping monster, leading into the darkness beyond.

Sophia pokes her head back outside and calls for Gabriel to join her. He scurries between the Sphinx's arms and stops beside her, panting and sweating.

"You ready?" Sophia asks.

"Yeah," Gabriel wheezes, catching his breath.

They slink through the cavernous lobby and into the passageway. As their eyes adjust to a deeper level of darkness, they find themselves surrounded by hundreds of dusty slot machines. Plastic cups and empty bottles are everywhere, both on the slot machines and the floor.

"Be careful," Sophia mouths, pointing out the ones on the floor.

She doesn't want Gabriel to kick a bottle or trip over a glass and cause a commotion.

But the four from the train are nowhere in sight. They are invisible in the darkness.

Sophia felt uneasy before, and that was when she could see them. Now they could be anywhere, surrounding the children, ready to ambush. A feeling of dread spreads through her chest. She doesn't care for this one bit.

Gabriel starts to speak, but Sophia swiftly brings a finger to her lips, and he falls silent. She can't see the others, but she does hear their movements far off in the darkness.

Suddenly, a voice calls out, and she almost yelps with surprise.

"Anybody think to bring a flashlight?" someone asks. The tone is high-pitched but undeniably male. Sophia thinks she hears a tinge of southern drawl.

"Yeah, I got one," says one of the women, and a beam of bluish light flickers to life. Immediately, a quartet of silhouettes becomes visible near the far end of the room.

That worked out nicely, thinks Sophia. The flashlight's bouncing beam will make following them a piece of cake. Plus, by contrast, she and Gabriel will be more difficult to notice in the dark—unless someone were to shine that beam directly at them, of course.

Now a third person, a man, speaks with the heavy accent of a European. He says, "We must find the southeast stairwell. Then we will be able to find the room."

Sophia raises an eyebrow. *The room?* What room? Have these people traveled across the country just to find something hidden in this huge pyramid? If so, what could they possibly be searching for?

The European speaks again and says, "Be on your guard. We don't know who might be watching."

A door opens at the far end of the casino floor, and pale daylight floods through it. Someone whoops with approval, like Sophia's dad used to do when the Steelers scored a touchdown, and the four file quickly through the doorway. With a metallic *clang,* the heavy door slams shut behind them.

"Hurry!" Sophia whispers, pulling Gabriel along by the hand. As they run, she slams her shin into the corner of a slot machine. She bites her lip to stifle a whimper of pain and hobbles on until they have reached the door.

"Ready?" she asks Gabriel.

Still squeezing her hand, Gabriel nods uncertainly.

Careful to make as little noise as possible, Sophia opens the door and ushers Gabriel through it.

They find themselves in a concrete stairwell. Although the day is young, the sunlight seeping through the translucent window is already turning it into an oven. From here, they have two choices: up to the higher levels of the casino, or down into the earth below.

"Which way?" Gabriel whispers.

Just then, something clatters below them, echoing up the stairwell. Muffled but irritated voices follow.

"I guess we're going down," Sophia answers nervously.

Daylight abandons them as they corkscrew down the winding staircase. The deeper they plunge, the deeper the darkness becomes. Soon Gabriel is little more than a phantom, an inky shadow moving at Sophia's side.

At least it isn't so stuffy down here, she tells herself.

After what feels like forever, they come to the bottom of the stairs. Here, marked with plentiful warning signs, an iron door blocks their way.

The door is old and roughhewn, quite out of place in a sleek and sophisticated casino. It also looks like it weighs a ton. Literally.

Sophia grabs one of the door's ancient rings. She yanks on it with all her might, but the door doesn't budge a single millimeter.

"Help me pull," she whispers to Gabriel.

Instead of helping, he laughs.

"What's so funny?" she asks curtly. Now isn't the time for jokes.

"It's already open!" Gabriel answers, pointing at the dark space along the door's edge. "It's just a crack, but I think we can fit."

Sophia goes first. The gap between door and wall is narrow, but she manages to squeeze through. The much smaller Gabriel follows without a problem.

As Sophia examines their new surroundings, she discovers they are at one end of a straight, dark tunnel. Unlike the rest of the building, its walls are rough and rocky. They look more like they belong inside a dragon's cave than a casino. At the other end of the corridor glows a bright disk of yellow light, partially eclipsed by four phantom-like silhouettes.

It's hard for Sophia to be certain from this distance, but they appear to be in a hurry.

The children creep along the subterranean tunnel, keeping close to the wall as they move through two hundred feet of darkness. Although they make no noise, Sophia feels like she is lighting off a cannon every time she exhales, and popping a balloon with each step she takes.

But no one hears them. Rather, as Sophia and Gabriel sneak further down the tunnel, the voices of the train people become audible.

"She has already been here," says the man with the European accent, and a curse word bursts from his lips. After a brief silence he explains, "The book isn't here anymore. See the empty pedestal in the middle of the map? And look at how the dust on the floor is disturbed.

Someone has been here very recently."

"Maybe the guardian?" suggests one of the women.

Sophia and Gabriel approach the end of the tunnel. A second iron door, so thick and ancient it could have stood at the entrance of a medieval castle, hangs open. On the other side is a vast, dome-shaped room. Sunlight filters in from somewhere far overhead. It fills the yawning chamber and illuminates what appears to be a large map spread from end to end across the floor.

It is this, the map on the floor, which all four of the train people are staring at.

The children are running out of darkness to hide them. They can't go any further without being seen, so Sophia directs Gabriel into the black space between the tunnel wall and the open iron door. Here they can hide and wait and listen.

"I do not think the Immovable did this," the accented man says in reply to the woman's question.

Sophia shows the darkness her most confused expression. What— or who—is an *Immovable?* Some sort of underground guardian? A security system? A monster?

The man continues, pointing at the ground and saying, "Look at these patterns in the dust. They swirl all around the room. Whoever was here last spent some time studying the map. An Immovable would have no reason to do so. Nor would they take the Book of Relics. According to my research, their only purpose is to guard the Hallowed Vaults and nothing else." There is a pause, then: "No, this must be the doing of Lin Lai and her people."

More people?

Until two nights ago, Sophia was sure she was the last person alive on planet Earth. Then Gabriel materialized on the roof of her van. The very next day, they found a train with four more people aboard.

And now this foreign man is claiming there is yet another gang of pyramid crashers somewhere nearby?

Everything Sophia has learned over the past couple years has flipped upside-down in less than forty-eight hours. With all the new information, a question sprouts inside her like a tiny sapling of hope.

How many more might be out there?

"Well, whaddya want us to do, boss?" asks the young man with the black hat and southern twang.

"Take pictures," the leader replies. "Take as many as you can and as fast as you can. If there *is* an Immovable around here, we will not want to linger."

The children overhear the clicking of cameras and the shuffling of feet. Through a tiny crack near the door's hinge, Sophia spots the dark-featured, suit-wearing man. He is kneeling, examining something on the ground. He reaches for it, rubs it gently with his fingers, and then stands up again.

"You do know what this means, don't you?" he asks the rest of the crew. "The fact that this place exists? It means the rest of the legend must also be real. It means this place—this room—is only the beginning. It means that if we are going to accomplish our goal, we will have to journey to the four corners of the earth. Are you prepared to do this? Are you ready for everything which lies ahead?"

"You know we're with you, Ettore," one of the women replies. "Your goal is our goal."

For a few minutes, nobody speaks. The only sounds coming from the room are those of the cameras, their shutters chattering as they record hundreds of pictures.

Eventually the leader declares, "That is enough. We should leave. If Lin has been here, we cannot waste another moment."

Sophia and Gabriel flatten themselves against the wall, holding their breath as the four file out. Now seeing the two women up close, Sophia thinks they are, in fact, twins. One has short-cropped hair, while the other wears hers in a long, single braid down the middle of her back. They are followed by their dark-featured leader, while the young man in the cowboy hat brings up the rear.

After the train people have gone a safe distance down the tunnel, Sophia and Gabriel scamper from their hiding place and into the room.

The chamber, Sophia notices, is about fifty feet across and perfectly circular. Its dome shape reminds her of the planetarium she visited in first grade. Unlike the rough tunnel, the walls and ceiling here are made of polished stone and are completely bare, devoid of any kind of decoration. The ceiling's one and only feature is the glass disk at its center, through which abundant sunlight pours into the room.

Now Sophia understands why the others were so fixated on the floor. Thousands—perhaps millions—of tiny tiles create the largest mosaic she has ever seen. Stretched from end to end, the sea of tiles covers the entire floor. Each stone square, which can't be any larger than her thumbnail, is one of two colors: white or black. All of them together form an unmistakable map of the world. The black tiles denote the presence of land, while the white ones make up lakes and rivers and oceans.

In the middle of the map, standing four feet high, is a stone pedestal. The smooth, circular platform on top is empty. According to the man called Ettore, something called the Book of Relics sat here until recently.

"What do you think the little red circles are for?" Gabriel whisper-yells at her.

He is squatting, studying a part of the map. As Sophia shuffles to his side, she realizes he is looking down at the American Southwest.

Below him, right where one would find Las Vegas, is a red circle the size of a dessert plate. It is made of a single tile and is sunk two inches lower than the rest of the floor.

Something else catches her eye, and she asks, "Can you move back just a bit?"

Gabriel remains in his squatting position as he scoots backward. When he does, two mysterious words become visible beneath the red circle.

Mappa Mundi.

"What's it mean?" asks Gabriel, tracing the letters with his fingers.

Sophia shakes her head and replies, "I don't know. It's in a different language. Latin, I think." Standing, she asks, "Are there any more like that?"

Gabriel shrugs. He is too fascinated with his first discovery to care.

It only takes a couple seconds for Sophia to find another red circle. This one is in the skinny part near the bottom of Central America, right before it balloons back out into South America—which is where she finds a third. As was the case with the first, each red circle has a pair of Latin words beneath it.

Templum Saltu. Summa Villa.

There is another red dot on the northernmost point of Europe—Norway? Sweden? Sophia cannot remember exactly. The script below it reads: *Promontorium Boreale.*

Deliberately, Sophia meanders around the whole map. As she does, she counts the red dots with their Latin subtitles. There are three in the Americas, two in Europe, one on the African mainland, and another on the large island east of the continent—Madagascar, she's pretty sure. Then there is an eighth just below the Arabian Peninsula and a ninth in the southeastern region of Asia, perhaps in India or China. It's difficult to know for sure because the map doesn't delineate borders between countries. Finally, she finds red dots on Japan, Australia, and in the middle of the ocean, far from the west coast of South America.

Including the Las Vegas dot, she counts twelve. A dozen locations scattered around the world, their meaning a complete mystery to her.

What, Sophia wonders, *did we stumble into?*

She certainly might have stayed to wonder some more. But at that moment, from the mouth of the tunnel, a rumbling *clang* echoes into the sunlit chamber.

Sophia jumps, startled, and peers into the darkness.

With a sickening realization, her stomach drops.

"Gabriel, come on! Hurry!" she cries.

Sophia doesn't wait for him. She sprints down the corridor as fast as her legs can carry her. At the other end, she runs into a dark and solid mass.

It's exactly as she feared. When the people from the train left, they shut the iron door behind them.

She throws all her weight against it, trying desperately to push it open. When Gabriel arrives, panting and frantic, he adds his meager strength to Sophia's efforts.

But the door will not budge. Not a single inch.

They are trapped.

Chapter Eight

ANTIKYTHERA

A MILLION CHILLING thoughts of starvation and dehydration, or of being ripped apart by cave monsters, flood Sophia's mind. All of them involve some version of she and Gabriel lying dead in this tunnel. For some reason she keeps thinking about Bixby all alone in the motorhome, who will slowly suffer a similar fate as he wonders why his mistress never returned for him.

Sophia doesn't have time to think through a plan. She has to act, even if that means taking desperate measures. Balling her hands into fists, she pounds the iron door as hard as she can. She screams. She shrieks. She punches and kicks. *Anything* which might attract the attention of the train people. Perhaps she and Gabriel will end up dead at their hands anyway, but she prefers those odds to an eternal entombment here.

Plus, in her jeans waistband, she still carries an ace-in-the-hole. She can't shoot her way through this door, but the four from the train might find her pistol a bit more persuasive.

Moments after Gabriel joins her in creating the racket, Sophia shushes him and puts her ear to the door.

Her plan has worked. She hears faint voices on the other side.

"Help!" she pleads, pounding once more to make certain they have heard her. "We're trapped inside. Please, open the door!"

A loud creak is followed by the grinding of metal upon stone, and the door begins to swing outward into the stairwell.

Sophia steps back and drops a hand to the butt of her pistol. She hopes she won't have to use it, but she must be prepared for every possibility.

After opening only a few inches, the door stops.

Through the narrow gap, the European asks, "Who are you? Are you one of the Immovables?"

"I don't even know what an Immovable is," she answers truthfully. "Look, we're just a couple of kids. We followed you here from Utah. Then when you shut the door, we got stuck back here."

"Lin's got kids working for her now?" one of the twins asks in disbelief. "She really will take anyone that'll have her."

"We don't know this Lin person," protests Sophia. "Honest. We saw your train when we were driving and followed you here. Please, let us out. We just want to go home."

She can't make out what the muffled voices say next, but it sounds as if they are having some sort of debate. She isn't certain, but she thinks she detects a note of concern. It's possible they trust her as little as she trusts them.

Louder, and with a tone of finality, the European tells the others, "We cannot linger here to debate this any longer. It is only a matter of time before our intrusion is discovered. We will take them to the train and deal with them there."

Deal with them? Sophia doesn't care for the sound of that. Her grip on the pistol tightens.

The European addresses them again. "We are opening the door, but I must insist that you come with us. Keep your hands behind your heads, and you will remain unharmed. Do we understand each other?"

Sophia struggles to find her voice as she answers with a simple "Yes."

She instructs Gabriel to do as ordered, then obediently puts her own hands—and a pistol—behind her head. Her heart pounds like a jackhammer in her chest. In her mind she plays out what will happen next and prays she won't have to squeeze the trigger.

The train people grunt as they strain to pull the heavy door. When the opening is wide enough, the European instructs them to slide through.

"You go first," Sophia whispers to Gabriel. The boy is whining, so she comforts him by adding, "Don't worry. I'm right behind you. I promise."

Careful to keep her pistol hidden, Sophia slips sideways through the gap with her back against the wall. A bright blue light all but blinds her as she arrives on the other side, and she winces against its light.

Although Sophia dreads what she must do, she knows she cannot hesitate without giving away her secret. At the moment, the element of surprise belongs to her, and she must use its every advantage if she and Gabriel will have any hope of escaping. She waits just long enough to make sure she is free and clear of the door, then jumps into action.

Quicker than a coffee-fueled gunslinger, Sophia whips the pistol from behind her head and trains it on the holder of the flashlight.

"Don't move!" she shouts, as the others, including Gabriel, jump back with cries of surprise. Because of the flashlight's intense beam in her face, she can't distinguish who's who, but as long as she keeps the pistol aimed in their general direction, they won't try anything funny.

She hopes.

"Please, put that down!" urges the European. "You do not understand—"

But Sophia isn't in the mood for bargaining. She cuts him off,
saying, "I'm not putting anything down. I'm the one with the gun."

One of the dark shadows holds up its hands, motioning for the
others to remain calm. Sophia guesses this is the European. Since he is
undoubtedly the leader of the gang, she aims the pistol at him.

"I want you all to get down on your knees," she instructs. "And
keep your hands in the air. Then me and Gabriel are gonna go up the
stairs. Don't follow us."

The European sinks slowly to his knees. The other two follow suit.
The other ... two?

Sophia doesn't even have time to finish her thought. Suddenly, her
arm is seized from behind and forced upward.

A bright flash and ear-splitting *CRACK!* rend the air at once. Bits
of the stairwell's concrete rain down from above, settling in her hair.

It seems everyone is shouting all at once as the pistol is wrenched
from her grasp.

An instant later, *she* is the one staring down the barrel.

The blond man with the black hat stands on the other end of it.
Blinded by the flashlight, she didn't realize there were only *three* of the
train people in front of her. The last one had been hiding in the darkness behind her.

"Nice try," Black Hat mutters darkly.

Now that Sophia is staring directly up into his face, she realizes he
can't be much older than seventeen or eighteen. His face is smooth
and handsome, and his skin a ruddy shade of brown, like the core of a
newly felled tree.

"Whaddya think we should do with 'em, Ettore?" he asks. "Stuff
'em back behind the door?"

"And leave them for the Immovable to find? Heavens, no!" replies the European, the one also called Ettore. "Even if it turns out they *are* Lin's people, I would never leave them to such an uncertain fate as that."

"Then what do we do with them?" asks the long-braided twin.

"Exactly as planned when we opened the door," answers Ettore. "We bring them with us to the train. But we must go *now*. If the Immovable did not already know we were here, that gunshot certainly alerted him."

The braided woman grabs Sophia's upper arm. Her fingers are a vise as she pushes the girl toward the stairs.

Beside and slightly behind her, Black Hat does the same with Gabriel, and the six of them hasten up the stairs toward the daylight. When they reach the top, they shuffle back through the open, dark room with the slot machines.

The Vegas heat slaps Sophia in the face as they emerge from the casino, and she instantly remembers how thirsty she is. She prays their captors are merciful enough to give her a glass of water once they are safely onboard the train.

Hurriedly, they pass the Sphinx' giant paws and the Bellagio's dusty fountains of old. They aren't on the wreck-studded Las Vegas Boulevard for long before both the train and the motorhome are in sight.

As Black Hat and Braid shove the children toward the train, Sophia hears Bixby's frantic cries. She looks up and sees him, paws on the motorhome's window, watching them nervously.

"Please!" she screams, desperation flooding her voice. "Please, let me get my dog! He's just over there in that motorhome. He'll die if you don't let me get him. Please!"

At first no one answers, and the braided twin continues pushing her toward the train. Then, to Sophia's surprise, the crop-haired woman steps defiantly in front of her sister.

"We aren't letting her dog die," she says in a steely tone. Then, gently, she tells Sophia, "Come with me."

Sophia is released without argument. She stumbles forward and into the other twin's much gentler grasp. At a half-run, the woman leads Sophia by the arm toward the motorhome. As soon as they reach it, Sophia unlatches the door.

Bixby explodes through it like a furry cannonball, knocking even Sophia backward. He is baring all forty-two of his angry teeth, and a deep growl rumbles in his throat. Sophia has never seen her friendly-to-a-fault dog act like this. Murder lurks in his eyes, and he is ready to kill. He advances upon the strange woman, muscles tensed and ready to spring. Bixby will defend his mistress even if it means taking the life of this intruder.

The woman lets go of Sophia and says, quite calmly, "Deal with him."

The girl kneels in front of her dog and scratches him behind the ears. At once, the furry bomb is defused. His whippy tail wags happily back and forth as he licks the salty sweat from Sophia's palm.

"Grab him, and let's go," the woman orders. She speaks gently but urgently. "We need to get to the train."

Sophia snags Bixby's leash from a hook inside the door. She has hardly used it the past couple years, and the dog cocks his head confusedly as she clips it to his collar. She wishes she had time to explain herself, but the moment the leash is secure, the woman tugs on her arm.

"To the train," she pleads. "We've wasted enough time."

They rush to the train's middle car. The moment they jump inside the door, there is a jolt, and the train starts moving.

Sophia takes in the new environment. It's obvious they are in a passenger compartment, but most of the seats have been torn out. Five mattresses, complete with sheets and pillows, have replaced them.

Gabriel is huddled upon one of the remaining seats, knees pulled up to his chest. Muffled whimpers escape his lips, and his wary eyes flit back and forth among the four adults.

The man in the suit beckons Sophia to take a seat next to Gabriel. She does, and Bixby lays his head on the boy's lap. Gabriel relaxes instantly and gives the dog a gentle scratch between the ears.

"Now then," the European begins, taking the seat across from them, "who are you, and why were you following us?"

Sophia looks at him with disgust and mistrust, like a four-year-old eyeing a large piece of steamed broccoli. She has no intention of telling him anything.

The man sighs. He pinches the corners of his eyes and rubs them, deep in thought. When he looks at her again, his expression is softer, and he says, "I am sorry for how things happened back there. We were in a hurry, and I did not know if we had time to explain our situation."

"And that makes kidnaping us okay?" Sophia challenges stubbornly. She glares into his dark-brown eyes.

The corners of his mouth twitch downward. "No," he says. "I suppose it does not. We will be happy to let you go once we are away from the city."

Black Hat steps forward in protest. "But what if they're Lin's people?"

In a chiding tone, the dark-featured man replies, "Micah, do you really think that is the case? Weigh the facts for a moment, and you will come to the very logical conclusion that they cannot belong to Lin. Why would they return to the map room after already beating us there? Would they not be hurrying as quickly as possible to the first destination? And why would they have driven here in a motorhome with a pet dog? It makes no sense. Lin works differently. You know that."

Black Hat, also known as Micah, chews the inside of his cheek as he analyzes the facts. He then shrugs, meanders to the compartment's rear, and flops contentedly onto a mattress.

Feeling bolder now, Sophia asks, "Who's Lin? We heard you talking about her when we were watching you."

The man grins warmly and says, "There will be time for that later. For now, let me introduce myself." He extends a hand and says, "My name is Ettore Majorana, and I am from Italy. On March 25, 1938, I was on a boat between Sicily and Naples when I slipped forward through time."

Sophia stares warily at his hand for a moment, then grabs it, gives it a brief shake, and says, "I'm Sophia Faraday. And the same thing happened to me and my dog on August 1, 2021."

She notices the twins share a brief look of shock. Then the braided one says, "I'm Kylah Alexander. And this is my sister, Kira." She jerks a thumb to indicate the identical face next to hers.

"We slipped forward the same day you did," Kira tells her, which explains their surprise. "We were in Charleston when it happened. South Carolina."

"Medina, Pennsylvania," Sophia informs them.

"And I was in Aiken, South Carolina," says the young man lying on the mattress. His fingers are laced behind his head, and the black hat covers his face. "November 14, 1978. Name's Micah Monroe."

"And then there is also Dario Fingir," Ettore informs them. "He is in the engine, operating the train. I found him while traveling through Spain."

At once, every eye falls upon the boy next to Sophia. She notices the sudden interest in him and says, "That's Gabriel. We only met each other two days ago."

With the warmth and sweetness of fresh-baked cookies, Ettore puts on his friendliest grin and says, "It is nice to meet you, Gabriel."

"Hi," the boy squeaks, barely meeting the other's gaze.

"And where did you come from?"

"Grand Junction," Gabriel answers. "In Colorado."

Sophia interjects and adds, "He actually didn't—well, he didn't jump ahead in time like the rest of us. He was there when everyone else disappeared around him."

Ettore Majorana meets her gaze. His mouth hangs open, betraying his disbelief, before he whispers, "He ... lived through it?"

Sophia nods.

"That is certainly remarkable," Ettore says, his voice low and pondering. "You are sure of it?"

Gabriel nods vigorously and answers, "Yeah. Everyone else disappeared and left me all alone—my mom, my sisters, my neighbors. It was really scary."

"I am sorry you had to go through that, Gabriel," says Ettore. He lays a comforting hand on the boy's shoulder. "I had a hard enough time surviving as a grown-up. I cannot imagine how difficult it was for a boy like you! How old were you? When they disappeared?"

"Six. It was my birthday."

"You must be very brave and strong," Ettore says brightly, "to have lasted so long on your own."

The boy beams proudly. He strokes Bixby's head with a renewed confidence.

But Sophia isn't so confident. Not yet, anyway. Clearing her throat, she asks, "How can we be sure *you* aren't the bad guys?"

Ettore chuckles at her forwardness and says, "You don't, I

suppose. But perhaps if I tell you our mission, I can convince you that we want the same thing you do."

Sophia doesn't say anything. She simply leans back and waits for more.

"Did you make it all the way into the map room?" Ettore asks.

Sophia nods.

"Then you also saw the *Mappa Mundi,* the 'Map of the World' spread across the floor," he continues. "Scattered around that map were twelve red dots, each of them with Latin words beneath. Did you see those?"

Again, Sophia nods.

"According to my research into some very credible sources," Ettore explains, "those red dots, besides the one specifying the map room itself, pinpoint eleven different locations. These are known as the Hallowed Vaults. Hidden within each vault is a single piece of an ancient and wonderful machine. When all of these pieces—or *relics*—are brought together and assembled, they create something called an Antikythera Device."

"A what?" interrupts Sophia, certain she misheard Ettore.

"*An-tee-kith-EER-uh,*" he repeats, this time stressing each syllable. "An Antikythera Device."

"What does it do?" asks Gabriel, suddenly interested in the conversation.

"Well, Gabriel," Ettore excitedly replies, "I only know rumors. But some have said that whoever owns the Antikythera Device will become master over Time."

Sophia exchanges a blank expression with Gabriel. If *she* doesn't get it, she certainly can't expect him to understand.

"Let me put it simply," Ettore says. "If we travel to all eleven of the Hallowed Vaults and find all eleven relics, we can assemble them and travel through time. Each of us can go back to our own eras. You will find your families, your friends. Do you understand?"

Sophia understands. She understands so well she can't speak. Ettore's revelation has overwhelmed her. Visions of birthday celebrations, of fishing at the creek with her brother Darius, of lazy Sunday afternoons, of her parents tucking her in and kissing her goodnight—they all fill her head at once. She gave up on these dreams, these fantasies, long ago. Could those fragmented memories become reality again?

"How do you know all this?" she asks, leery of the too-good-to-be-true revelation.

Ettore seems taken aback by the prying question, but he gives a low laugh and answers, "It is a long story. Let's just say that one of the most protected libraries in the world, the one below the Vatican in Rome, is not protected any longer. For over a thousand years those shelves have held many of the world's greatest and most powerful secrets. I happened to discover the writings about this one. The presence of the map room, I believe, confirms its truth."

Ettore notices Gabriel licking his cracked and dry lips. Addressing the twins, he asks, "Would you please bring them some water? They look like they are about to collapse."

Again, Sophia is at a loss for words. Her mind is an overloaded circuit, too burdened with incoming information to output a reply. This man's story sounds like a book she might have read long ago, before she slipped through time and her entire world changed. A race around the world, collecting ancient artifacts? A shadowy villain named Lin Lai? A band of once-strangers who become closer than family? It all sounds like the adventure of a lifetime!

But she is so young, and Gabriel even younger. Plus, she has Bixby to think about. How well would a dog do traveling around the world?

There is a comfortable home waiting for her in Denver. With her motorhomes, she already has two continents she can explore. Isn't that enough?

It also strikes her then that no one has invited them on this epic quest. Perhaps it's still their plan to cut the children loose and continue on their own as soon as they have the opportunity.

Kylah disrupts Sophia's thoughts as she hands her a water bottle. Sophia passes it to Gabriel, allowing him to drink first. The boy greedily sucks it down. Only backwashed dregs remain when he returns the bottle to Sophia.

The glimmer of a grin flashes across Kira's face as she offers the girl a second bottle.

By the time Sophia is finished drinking, she has made up her mind.

"Can we come with you?" She blurts the question before she has time to second-guess herself. "To find this Anky—Anti—whatever it's called?"

Ettore raises a doubting eyebrow.

"Antikythera," he says, supplying the word she cannot remember. "And I do not know if that is a wise idea. The journey will be full of dangers, both from people and from Mother Nature. Neither I nor anybody else could promise your safety. It will be challenging, even for adults such as us. And not just physically, but also mentally and emotionally."

He pauses, weighing her request in the scales of his mind. "I must have time to think about this, and we must all discuss the matter together," he says, indicating the rest of his crew.

"Okay," Sophia mumbles feebly. His hesitance is more disappointing than she would have guessed.

Abruptly changing the subject, Ettore asks, "Where do you live? We could all use a bit of rest and a break from this stuffy train."

"Just outside of Denver," she replies.

There is no mistaking the delighted gleam in Ettore's twinkling eyes.

"That," he says, "is exactly where we are headed."

Chapter Nine

STARS AND SPACE-TIME

AN IMPRESSED WHISTLE SLIDES through Micah's teeth, and he exclaims, "Sure picked a beauty of a castle for yourself, didn't ya!"

He gawks at the marble-floored foyer as he enters Sophia's house with the rest from the train. Overhead hangs a magnificent chandelier whose dangling crystals project a thousand rainbows onto a regal staircase.

"I guess I have fancy tastes!" Sophia replies cheerily. "When I was little, our house was tiny, and I always wanted a huge one like this. I'm glad it'll be filled with people for a change!"

When Sophia first came to Genesee, a ritzy town nestled in the foothills above Denver, this palatial home was the fanciest one she could find. For a while, she felt like a princess coming home to her castle. But lately her "castle" has seemed cold and hollow. After living in the multimillion-dollar mansion for two years, she no longer appreciates its cedar-and-granite grandeur the way she once did.

One of Sophia's wall decorations, a framed sheet of ancient brown paper, catches Micah's attention. He can't hide his surprise as he stammers, "Is that *the* Declaration of Independence? Like, the original?"

Sophia reddens with guilt and says, "Yeah. I didn't think anyone would care."

Micah beams with admiration for her spunk and asks, "What else ya got in here? Rosetta Stone? Ark o' the Covenant?"

She giggles and replies, "No, not those. Not yet, anyway. But there's lots of other cool stuff I've set up around the house. You can wander around and look if you want."

"Thank you for having us, Sophia," Ettore says cordially. "We appreciate your hospitality."

Sophia can't help but speculate about the beat-up suitcase he carries at his side. Though he never seems to open it, she's noticed that he always keeps it close. Even in the train's tight quarters, he either held it on his lap or placed it on the floor firmly between his feet.

What could possibly be inside that's so valuable? she wonders.

But such questions will have to wait until later. Presently, the half-light of early evening filters through the home's high windows. She knows it will be dark before long, so she tells the others, "You can find whatever room you want to sleep in. You'll probably be able to tell which one is mine. But we'll need electricity for showers and lights tonight, so I'm gonna get the generator running."

As Sophia exits through the spacious kitchen and into the four-car garage, she overhears a squeal of girlish excitement.

"I can't remember the last time I had a shower!" Kylah delightedly exclaims.

Though no one can see it, Sophia grins. During the past twenty-four hours, she has fallen in love. This strange collection of people from two different continents certainly terrified her at first, but once they put their misunderstandings and suspicions aside, it amazed her how quickly they started feeling like family.

The twins, Kylah and Kira Alexander, may look alike but are

complete opposites. Kylah is sunny and upbeat, while Kira is a calming blend of reserved and serious, sad and kind. The first is a puppy, the second a cat.

Then there is Micah. Gabriel still doesn't trust him after his rough handling in Las Vegas, but Sophia finds him entertaining. He makes jokes—most of them so corny she cringes—whenever he can. He has the wide, toothy smile of a cartoon character, and it doesn't take much for him to display it. He and the twins were the first of the group to band together. Almost a year ago they stumbled upon one another, and the three have been together ever since.

Dario Fingir is the only one Sophia doesn't care for, but she supposes that every family has its obnoxious uncle. Dario is foul-mouthed and as ill-tempered as a sunburned rattlesnake. She prefers him operating the train, where he stays far away from the rest of them. Ettore constantly apologizes for the Spaniard and claims she'll warm up to him sooner or later.

Sophia isn't so confident.

Then there is Ettore himself. The suit-loving Italian is gentle, calm, and affable. Although he appears to be in his thirties, the bronze-skinned ringleader has an almost grandfatherly aura about him. Perhaps it's the way he takes time to talk to shy, nervous Gabriel, or how he quietly reads his dusty books with a contented grin. Whatever the case, it has taken only a day for him to steal her heart entirely.

They've known each other such a short time, but Sophia knows she will do anything to hold on to this feeling, because it's the feeling of family. It's the feeling of belonging. Of acceptance. Of friendship. It's a feeling she hasn't experienced for ages. A feeling she never expected to have again.

Once the generator is running and pumping electricity into the house, Sophia returns indoors. There are five showers in the mansion, and it isn't long before all are in use. As Sophia herself rinses away the sweat and grime of the last few days, she feels reborn, like when a reptile sheds its old skin and clothes itself in a new one. She's an altogether different person, with a fresh life and a future full of infinite and exciting possibilities.

At twilight, Sophia butchers three of her precious chickens. Kylah and Kira combine the tender filets with tomatoes from the garden and dried herbs to create a mouth-watering main course. With it they serve a steaming pot of buttery mashed potatoes, and everybody eats until they are stuffed.

After dinner, on a table tennis-sized television, they watch *Star Wars*—Micah's pick. He hadn't yet seen the groundbreaking movie before he slipped five decades forward in time.

The only one who doesn't watch the whole movie is Dario. He grunts his disapproval after only five minutes and retreats upstairs to bed. Gabriel, whose parents thought he was too young to see it, watches the entire movie open-mouthed and unblinking.

"I'm going to bed," Kira announces when the movie's final credits start rolling.

"I'm with you," her twin announces. After peeling herself from the leather sofa, she turns to Sophia and says, "Thanks for the shower and the chickens, Soph. Goodnight, everyone!"

The twelve-year-old's heart flutters. Now she even has a nickname.

"May the Force be with you," Micah quips dreamily as he exits behind the twins.

"Are you going to bed too?" Gabriel asks Ettore.

The Italian pats a timeworn, leather-bound book sitting on the sofa beside him and replies, "I think, perhaps, I will stay up and read a while."

"What's the book about?" Gabriel inquires.

"Old tales and rumors about the Antikythera Device," Ettore answers plainly. "I do not know how much is real and how much is legend. Usually the truth is somewhere in the middle, but some of it may end up being quite useful."

Out of nowhere, Gabriel asks, "Do you think I can find my mom and dad again?"

Ettore winces like he's been stung by a bee. The faintest shimmer of tears gives his eyes a glassy sheen as he replies, "I hope so, Gabriel. I hope so more than anything."

"Me too," the boy says. Then, without another word, he hops off the sofa and leaves.

Bixby totters alongside him, and together they head upstairs to bed.

"I turn off the generator at night," Sophia says, also rising from her couch seat, "so I don't know how long you'll be able to read. I've got it connected to a battery, so there's always some power left in the system afterward, but the lights'll go out once that's dead."

"It is no problem," Ettore replies with his genial grin. "Thank you, and goodnight."

After shutting down the generator, Sophia heads upstairs to her bedroom. She has decorated it to be as homey and cozy as possible. Pictures of her family hang on the walls, most of them from summer vacations. Every year, they would decide as a family where to go. For a whole week, they enjoyed each other's company, usually somewhere they could camp, fish, and escape from the loud and busy world.

As she looks at them now, her mother's kind eyes stir together the emotions of sorrow and warmth in her breast. Her dad's rugged, handsome face makes her feel both safe and lonely all at once. Her grinning brothers Darius and Eric, one older and one younger, stare out at her through the pane of class. She remembers how some days with them were perfect, while on others she wished she could kill them.

Now she would kill even to have the "kill them" days back.

In her private bathroom, Sophia brushes her teeth for three full minutes, just like her dentist mom taught her. Then she slips under her bedcovers and switches off the lamp.

Maybe it's too weird trying to sleep without Bixby next to her, or maybe it's because the quilt she always snuggled with—the one her mom made—stayed in Vegas with the motorhome. Whatever the reasons, Sophia tosses and turns for close to an hour, until she hears the hum of electricity in the walls pop and then die in silence. Fifteen sleepless minutes later she is out of bed again, navigating her way carefully through the dark hallway, down the stairs, out the front door, and into the chilly night air.

Wearing her fuzzy socks, she shuffles down the front walk and driveway. There she stops and cranes her neck heavenward.

The electric band of the Milky Way stretches above her like the trillion-mile tentacle of some immense space squid. She feels both infinitesimally small and larger than life as she holds the galaxy's billion stars in her marble-sized eyes.

"It is beautiful, no?"

A sharp cry of surprise escapes Sophia's lips when she hears the voice.

She is not alone as she thought.

"I'm sorry!" Ettore exclaims from nearby. "I thought you followed me and knew I was here. The lights went out, so I stepped outside for some fresh air before bed."

"No, it's—I'm okay," Sophia assures him, even though her heart is playing xylophone on her ribs.

"Do you come out here often at night?" he asks.

"Yeah, pretty much whenever I can't sleep. I'd watch TV probably, but it's too much work to get the generator going again, especially in the dark."

Both man and girl stare upward in silence.

Then Sophia asks the question that's been nagging her for more than two years.

"What do you think happened to us?"

Ettore stares at her. "What do you mean?"

"Why did we slip forward through time? How did it happen?"

Ettore doesn't answer her directly. Instead he asks, "Did you know I was one of the brightest physicists in the world during the 1930s?"

Sophia stares at him blankly.

"It's true," he promises, with the quaver of a chuckle in his voice. "At least, the brightest one of my age. I have read there were even subatomic particles named after me, ones I had theorized before my disappearance. My point is not to boast, but to say that of all the people who might be left on this planet, you could not have asked your question of a more knowledgeable person than myself."

He pauses, frowning, then says, "But all I have are theories, and not even those, really. It is probably more honest to call them guesses. The truth is that time has acted in a way neither I nor anyone else could have predicted. Time flows along, and we flow through it, correct? This has always been the way of the universe. But we human beings failed to realize something: just because something always *has been* a certain way, this does not mean it must always *continue* in that same way."

"Sorry," interrupts Sophia. "I'm not following."

"We thought time would continue flowing a certain way because it always *has* flowed a certain way—according to humanity's limited knowledge, at least," Ettore explains. "Do you understand that?"

Sophia nods.

Ettore continues. "Then the normal flow of time changed—for some of us anyway—almost like a stream running into a large rock. Most of the stream goes one direction, while a small part breaks off in another. At some point, you and I and the others broke away from the mainstream, while the rest of the world continued along the normal flow of time."

"Okaaaaay," says Sophia uncertainly. She understands his words, but she doesn't know what his point is.

"I believe that the 'rock' in our time stream was the Sun," says Ettore. "More specifically, I think intense and rapid changes in the Sun's mass ripped holes in the fabric of space-time. This caused some of us to slip away from the normal flow of time and forward into the present."

"Whoa, slow down," says Sophia. "The fabric of space-time? What's that?"

Ettore ponders how he can communicate the idea, then illustrates by saying, "Imagine four people holding the four corners of a bed-sheet so that it is stretched very tight. Physical space and time are like the fibers of that sheet, all woven together and holding strong."

"Okay," mutters Sophia, trying her hardest to follow him.

"Now imagine that a bowling ball is placed into the middle of that sheet," continues Ettore. "The fibers near the bowling ball are now pulled further apart than the fibers near the four corners of the sheet, because that is where they are under the greatest strain. Now imagine that somebody throws a handful of debris onto the sheet—sand, pebbles, sticks, and leaves. Will the pebbles, sticks, and leaves be able to pass through the stretched fibers to the other side of the sheet?"

Sophia shakes her head and answers, "Probably not."

"Correct," says Ettore. "But what about the smallest particles of sand? Might *they* pass through to the other side?"

The long illustration suddenly clicks for Sophia. "Yes," she replies, "some of them probably would."

"That is what I think happened to us," concludes Ettore. "I believe there were a few places where the fibers of space-time were stretched too wide, allowing people, who are relatively small in the cosmic scheme of things, to slip through. Again, it is just a theory, but I do believe this could explain our present situation."

"But what about everyone else?" Sophia asks. "The billions of people that were on Earth? Could the fabric have stretched enough to let *all* of them slip to a different period in time?"

"That is what I was hinting toward when I first began talking about space-time," the physicist answers. "Go back to the bowling ball. What if the ball began rapidly changing its weight, becoming heavier and lighter and heavier and lighter. What would happen?"

"I guess it would start bouncing up and down," Sophia responds after a moment's thought, "and maybe even tear the sheet."

"Precisely. Then much more would pass through to the other side—maybe not the entire earth, but perhaps all of puny humankind."

"But how could that happen?" Sophia asks. "I mean, with the sun? How could it gain and lose mass that fast?"

"Again, this is all theory," Ettore answers, "but if there were great ejections in the form of solar flares, the sun could lose great amounts of mass very quickly. Then, if the sun's own gravity pulled most of that mass back into itself, it regains that mass—again, very quickly. During an especially active period of this, the damage to space-time might have been enough to send humanity away from the normal flow of time to somewhere else. Some*time* else."

"And this ... Antikythera Device," Sophia deduces, finally con-
necting all the dots. "You think it can make those holes too? Holes
that let us travel through time?"

Ettore offers her a sheepish grin and says, "I know what it sounds
like. But yes, I do. And it won't be random travel, random slips to
goodness-knows-where. The Antikythera Device will allow for *controlled* time travel. If it works, it means we all go home again."

"But in order to find the different pieces of the Device, you need
that Book of Relics thing. Right?"

"It would certainly help," Ettore says, "although I do not think it
is one hundred percent necessary. There are other clues which could
lead us to the general locations of the relics. The Latin phrases below
the red dots, the ones you saw in the map room, provide such clues.
Many of the books I've read give hints as well."

"So why do you need the Book of Relics?" asks Sophia.

"Right now we are a bit like people grasping around a dark cave,"
replies Ettore. "We don't know the relics' exact locations, nor do we
even know what they will look like. The book would answer many of
those questions, allowing us to obtain the relics much more quickly.
Without it, the search could take many days at any one of those eleven
locations."

"Will you let me and Gabriel go with you?" Sophia blurts the question before she can stop herself, even though she already knows what
Ettore's answer will be.

"I cannot make that decision on my own," he replies. "Tomorrow,
I will discuss it with my people. But I *can* promise you this: even if we
do not bring you to find the relics, I will come back for you when our
task is done. I *will* bring you home again."

The Italian physicist rubs his chilled arms and says, "Let's return indoors. We both need sleep. Tomorrow is an important day!"

Inside, Ettore says goodnight and retreats to his bedroom. Sophia returns to her own bed and burrows under the warmth of her covers. Comforted by Ettore's answers to her many questions, she falls immediately asleep.

Chapter Ten

THE FIRST DEATH

SOPHIA'S EYES POP OPEN the next morning when Bixby jumps on her and aggressively licks her chin. Giggling, she shoves his face away from hers. She notices that Gabriel is there too, standing at the foot of her bed and grinning at Bixby's tongue-attack.

"Morning, Gabe," Sophia greets him sleepily.

She notices something different about him. It takes her foggy brain a few seconds to realize that someone has given him a haircut since last night. The long, stringy locks have been chopped away, leaving only close-cut, wavy hair on his head.

"Your hair looks nice," she adds.

"Thanks," Gabriel replies. "Kira cut it for me."

"What time is it?" asks Sophia.

Gabriel looks embarrassed. Even though he is staring at the clock on her nightstand, he says, "I don't know."

Sophia suddenly wants to cry for him. He wasn't even old enough to tell time when everyone left him.

When she glances at the clock, she jumps out of bed.

"It's already ten?" she exclaims. "Ugh! Why do I keep sleeping in so late! What's everyone else doing?"

"Actually," says Gabriel, "they're having a meeting. They sent me upstairs so I wouldn't hear what they were talking about."

Any lingering drowsiness vanishes instantly as Sophia says, "They're talking about *us*. Whether or not they're gonna take us with them. Come on!"

Sophia tells Bixby to stay in her bedroom, then tiptoes down the stairs. Gabriel trails behind. He looks confused about the sneaking around until Sophia tells him, "We need to listen in and spy on them. Are they in the big living room? Where we watched *Star Wars?*"

Gabriel nods.

They creep like ninjas from the bottom of the stairs to the corner that separates kitchen from living room. They can't get any closer than this without being seen, so they hide there, out of sight, and strain their ears to listen to the voices in the next room.

They hear Kylah first as she asks, "Why Norway?" She merely sounds curious, not challenging. "Shouldn't we head south? The closest piece looks like it's in Mexico."

"Because," replies Ettore, "Lin will be going to Norway."

"How do you know?" asks Dario. Unlike Kylah, his tone *is* challenging.

"We were together, just the two of us, for over a year," says Ettore. "I know how she thinks. Considering this is already the end of August, it makes sense to go to Norway now, before fall and winter set in. The Latin words we saw in the map room, *Promontorium Boreale,* mean 'North Cape.' It refers to the most northerly point of Europe at the furthest tip of Norway. We do not want to find ourselves hundreds of miles above the Arctic Circle in the dead of winter. If we don't go now, we may be forced to wait many months. Lin knows this too. That is where she will go first."

"Couldn't we try for the other half of the relics?" asks Micah. "Let Lin go through the trouble of finding some for us? Maybe we could work something out with her later on."

"Wishful thinking," Ettore replies. "Lin is not the kind of person to cooperate. Nor would I want to make a deal. Her goal is much too different—too *sinister*—for us to compromise. The only way this works is if we beat her and retrieve the relics before she does."

Nobody argues the point further during the short pause that follows.

"Then," continues Ettore, "we have no more time to lose. Lin is already ahead of us. I am sure of it."

What the Italian says next cuts Sophia to pieces.

"We must say our goodbyes to the children and be on our way."

Sophia can't believe what she's hearing. The twisting blade of his words pierces her gut. The sky-high hopes, the promise of adventure and purpose and belonging, are suddenly nothing more than the fragmented remains of a smashed mirror.

Her heartbreak is replaced quickly by rage. Flying around the corner and into full view of the others, Sophia cries out, "Are you serious? You can't leave us behind! You—you just can't!"

As if he half-expected her to be eavesdropping, Ettore fixes his calm gaze on her. He says, "I am truly sorry. We already discussed the matter. The majority does not believe it wise to bring two children with us. And, I admit, I am one of them."

Sophia starts to protest, but Ettore's raised voice drowns hers out. "The dangers will be too real, the difficulties too great. I am sorry, Sophia. Truly, I am. But it is for the best."

The girl can say nothing in reply. Her words are lost in disappointment and sorrow. What will they do now? Sit back for weeks, then months, then years, hoping and praying that Ettore and his friends might—*might*—fulfill their self-imposed quest to build the Antikythera Device? Even if they did, would they delay traveling back to their own time periods, their own families, in order to journey thousands of miles back to two waiting children?

Kira is visibly upset by the verdict. She says, "For the record, I don't agree with this decision at all. It's not right to leave two kids on their own like this."

"Feel free to stay with them," snaps Dario, standing in the corner of the TV room. His arms are crossed, and a dark shadow has settled over his face. "Replace the two you lost."

Sophia doesn't know what Dario is talking about, but she does see a distinct change in Kira's expression. Her stony demeanor grows ugly and vicious, like that of a lioness robbed of her cubs. Even her voice mimics a lioness as she growls, "You nasty piece of—"

"Kira, Dario," Ettore interrupts, "not now. Save your quarrel for the train."

Dario shrugs and stares at his feet. Even he knows he crossed a line.

"He's always baiting her," argues Kylah, coming to her sister's defense. "I say leave *him* here!"

"Good luck operating the train," Dario snipes back at her. His upper lip is curled into a snarl.

"All of you, *please!*" Ettore admonishes them. "We simply do not have time for this. With every moment we waste here, Lin gains more ground on us."

"I believe what Ettie is trying to say," Micah calmly suggests, again sporting his black hat, "is if we don't learn to play nice together, Miss Lai's gonna win the game. Which means we all lose."

Ettore seems satisfied with Micah's explanation of the matter, and he again faces Sophia. He appears mortified with himself as he says, "I know I have no right to ask this of you, but I need a favor."

Sophia glares at him, still fighting back tears. "Okay. What?"

"Can we please borrow the white van in the garage. To take us back to the train? Perhaps you could pick it up there later. After we have gone."

Her steely anger collapses into weary hopelessness. She shrugs and says, "Yeah. Fine. Key's hanging on the fridge."

The time it takes them to leave her home is both eternal and instantaneous. Sophia sits on the sofa and stares at the television screen, dazed, unable to believe their new friends are abandoning them. She tries consoling herself with the reminder that she at least has Gabriel, but she finds little comfort in the fact. It's like thinking she won the lottery, only to have someone hand her a five-dollar bill. Everything feels unfair. Cruel, even.

As the rest of Ettore's crew brings their belongings into the garage, Micah approaches Sophia.

"For what it's worth," he says, "I voted to let you come. In the two days I've known you, you've shown more wit and nerve than I'd expect from someone twice your age. It's a shame we won't have you along. But we'll come back for you when this is all over. I'll get you home again or die trying. See ya, Soph."

After the rest come to offer their goodbyes, silence fills the mansion. Sophia doesn't know how long she sits there in her wordless stupor, tears dripping silently from her stinging eyes. She hardly notices when Bixby peels himself from Gabriel's side to lay his comforting head on her lap.

When Gabriel asks a short while later if he can watch something on the television, she sets it up for him.

But she feels dead inside, like a zombie. She has a heartbeat and a pulse but is empty of everything else.

Halfway through some movie about dragon training she has never watched, Sophia tells Gabriel, "I'm going out to feed the chickens and check the garden. I'll be back in a bit."

Outside, she breathes in the fragrance of the backyard pines. It's a scent that has always brought peace and comfort to her lonely heart.

Not today, though.

The chicken enclosure lies a short distance downhill from the house, bordering the first trees of the forest. When she sees the birds strutting about their pen, she can't stop herself from hating them. She had been planning to release them before leaving with Ettore's crew. Now she will have to feed them until she dies, stuck here in her mansion prison while the adventure of a lifetime is enjoyed by others.

She sighs. She knows she shouldn't be so dramatic, but the disappointment is fresh.

A grain bucket sits outside the wire fence. Sophia opens the lid, then uses a large metal scoop to rain the grain mixture—oats, corn, barley—onto the floor of the enclosure. Like crazed, feathered piranhas, the chickens streak toward her from every corner of the coop. Together they greedily gobble down their meal.

Deafened by the symphony of squawking and clucking, Sophia almost doesn't hear Gabriel's screams.

"Help! Help! Sophia! Help!"

The hairs prickle on the back of her neck. Goosebumps crawl down her flesh.

Gabriel's shouts are followed by Bixby's frantic, growling barks.

Another voice joins theirs, floating upon the air. A man's voice. Micah? Ettore? No. This one is too steely. Snarling and vicious.

Sophia drops the grain scoop and sprints up the hill. Instinctively, she reaches to her hip, but the pistol isn't there. She feels sick as she remembers that Micah never gave it back.

But who could be attacking Gabriel? she wonders. Have they been tracked down by the enigmatic Lin Lai, whose name Sophia has heard a dozen times, but whose story she knows so little about?

She bounds up the steps, bursts through the back door, sprints across the kitchen.

And stops dead in her tracks.

Gabriel's shirt is balled up in the fist of a wiry old man. A gnarled, gray mane tumbles down his shoulders and back like swamp moss hanging from an ancient oak. His forest-green shirt is streaked with filth, and his khaki pants are frayed and sun bleached.

Sophia, however, notices none of these features. Her attention is fixed on the nine-inch hunting knife clutched in the man's hand.

"Where are the rest, boy?" he demands. His tone is low and threatening. "I saw you in Las Vegas, so don't bother denying it. Tell me where they are!"

The blade is so close to Gabriel's mouth, his breath is fogging the steel.

"I—I don't know!" he yells. Tears pour from his wide and terrified eyes. "They went back to the train. They're—they—left us!"

"Then why were you calling for help?" growls the man, pressing the knife's edge to Gabriel's neck. "You're a liar. Let me show you what happens to lying little boys!"

Sophia has no time to think. She charges forward with no strategy, no plan but to punch, kick, and claw for as long as she can put up a fight.

As she rushes toward the murderous man, she realizes she will probably die. Too late, though. She is committed. If anything, she hopes to buy enough time for Gabriel to slip away and escape.

From the corner of his eye, the man catches sight of Sophia barreling down on him. Instinctively, he whirls about, slashing the blade in a vicious downward arc.

Too soon. The knife slices only the air.

The poor timing of the attack is what saves Sophia's life. She tackles the man and slams him into the wall with all the force of an enraged hockey player. The knife flies from the man's bony fingers, clatters against the wall, and drops onto the hardwood floor. Their bodies follow. Sophia punches, elbows, gouges—whatever her unskilled, untrained impulses tell her to do.

But the old man is smarter, more experienced, and surprisingly strong. He wrestles his younger opponent into submission until Sophia's back is flat against the ground.

His arthritic hand finds the knife, and he raises it high.

"Pleasepleaseplease—nononono," Sophia pleads. She grabs the man's wrist and pushes against it with all her strength.

The man leans his weight into the blade. Sophia resists, but her muscles are shaky, weakening, unable to stop what is coming.

Slowly, slowly, slowly, the blade sinks toward her. It is an instrument of death she can delay but not stop.

Sophia fights against the oncoming tears. She doesn't want to die crying.

It is then, in the moments before her impending death, that she notices the tattoo on the man's wrist. The ink is faded, but still clear enough to make out the details of an ornate letter *I* written in some kind of fancy Latin script. As the knife inches toward Sophia's chest, the tattoo approaches with it.

Sophia imagines the blade sinking into her chest. Hundreds—*thousands*—of thoughts flash through her mind like a movie in fast-forward. She wonders how much it will hurt to die. She wonders whether it will take a long time for the darkness to creep over her and claim her forever. She wonders whether the man will kill Gabriel too, and if their souls, their spirits, will be together once it's all over.

But Sophia never gets her answers.

The knifepoint is only a millimeter from her chest when a deafening *CRACK!* fills the room. As if punched by some invisible hand, the man jerks and tumbles to Sophia's side.

He doesn't move again.

"Jeez! You alright, Soph?" a familiar voice asks her.

Dazed and trying to process what's happening, Sophia looks away from the dead fellow toward the speaker.

Micah stands on the far side of the room. A pistol—*her* pistol—is held firmly in his hand. From its barrel, a wisp of black smoke curls upward, where it disappears into the air.

Chapter Eleven

AN UNEXPECTED PILOT

"HEY! YOU ALRIGHT?" Micah asks again. He approaches Sophia slowly, like she's some wounded animal he doesn't want to spook.

"I—I'm—" Sophia stutters. She wants to tell him she is fine, but the lie sticks in her throat. Instead of words, tears of relief come spilling out. Within moments, full sobs break through the floodgates, and she covers her eyes. Her chest hurts so badly, she wonders if the man didn't stab her after all.

She senses a presence beside her, a pair of muscled arms pulling her close. However long she cries, she doesn't know. She can't remember the last time she let herself show this kind of vulnerability. It feels like weakness, but it also feels good. Like when she was a little girl, sick with fever, and her mom rocked her and sang to her.

Sophia eventually opens her eyes. Kira—stoic Kira—is the one holding her. Gabriel stands between Bixby and Ettore, staring at her in shock. Dario, Micah, and Kylah are lined up behind them, gazing at the grisly scene and the dead man at the center of it.

Removing a quilt from the sofa, Ettore drapes it over the old man's body. When he is satisfied every inch of him is covered, he steps back.

"Wh-why ... did you ... come back?" Sophia asks, her words garbled by emotional sobs.

"Someone blew up our train," Kira answers, stroking the nape of her neck.

"And they did it with *my* dynamite," Dario adds with a scowl. He seems more distraught over the loss of his explosives than over Sophia's near-miss with death. Shifting his bulky black duffel from one hand to the other, he says, "At least I had the good sense not to keep it all in one place."

Kira rolls her eyes at him and returns her attention to Sophia. "We were worried they might've tracked us back to your house. We were right. Got here just in time."

"Kira, will you take her upstairs, please?" Ettore says. "Gabriel too. We will remove the body and clean up."

Kira leads them to Sophia's bedroom. Bixby follows and jumps onto the bed alongside his mistress.

Burying her face in the dog's wiry fur, Sophia sobs until she has emptied herself of every emotion.

"I'll go downstairs and make sure they're finished," Kira says. "You'll be okay for a minute?"

Sophia nods and snuffles. With the back of her hand, she wipes away the tears.

When Kira is gone, Gabriel says in his small, squeaky way, "Thanks. For saving me. I thought he was gonna kill me."

Sophia wraps an arm around his shoulder and hugs him to her side. "I'm glad I got there in time," she replies, leaning her head against his.

"Were you scared?" he asks.

"*So* scared," she answers, vaguely amused at his innocent question. "But I was mostly scared he would hurt you and Bixby. I'm glad we're safe now."

"Maybe we should've never followed the train," Gabriel casually suggests.

"Yeah," Sophia mutters. "Maybe."

After this, they sit in silence until Kira returns.

"They're finished," she says. "It's safe to come down again."

The rest of Ettore's gang have made themselves comfortable in the sitting room on the south side of the house. When the children enter with Kira, Ettore stands and offers them his own seat.

"Are you alright?" he asks. Fatherly concern creases his features.

"Yeah," Sophia answers.

But she knows she will see the man again in her dreams. Probably next to the old woman from Asheville.

A nervous tension hangs over the room, as if somebody just died—which is indeed what happened, Sophia remembers.

Finally, she asks, "Who was that? One of Lin Lai's people?"

"Nah," Micah answers, his smile thin-lipped and grim. "Lin's pretty awful, but killing a couple kids in cold blood ain't exactly her style."

"That man was an Immovable," Ettore confidently informs them. "I noticed the letter *I* tattooed on his wrist. That is one of their marks. He must have tracked us through Las Vegas, then followed us here. It is even possible he was hiding on our own train."

"But what *is* an Immovable?" Sophia asks. She figures if she fills her brain with questions and answers, these will distract her from the trauma of the previous hour.

"They're a kind of guardian," Kylah explains, fiddling with the end of her long braid. "Security guards for the Antikythera Device. Ettore's read about them."

"Yes, but we do not know much," the physicist adds. "The Immovables are a mystery, mostly. They have been around for centuries.

Maybe longer. They have sworn their lives to protecting the various pieces of the Antikythera Device, making sure they are never found and never brought together. And, apparently, there was also one keeping watch over the map room."

"Hardly matters anymore," Dario interjects sourly. "By now Lin has a significant head start, and it'll take days to prepare another train. So unless one of you knows how to fly an airplane, we'll never be able to catch up."

"Actually," Sophia slyly retorts, "I might be able to help with that."

Six curious heads turn, giving her their full attention.

She stands and says, "Follow me."

Sophia leads them to the basement and turns on the lights. The expansive room is carpeted and fully furnished with sofas, easy chairs, a pool table, a ping-pong table, and another huge television with all sorts of video game hookups. In a plexiglass display case, a pair of ruby slippers sits between a blue sapphire and a trio of gem-studded rings.

But it is the white ovoid capsule sitting in the far corner which commands their attention. It appears large enough to fit at least two people inside, like an egg laid by some mammoth, prehistoric chicken.

Sophia opens a narrow door in its side, revealing an interior with two chairs, a video screen, and an intricate control panel. Printed in metallic blue letters above the door are the words *Aero-7 Flight Simulator*.

"If you're looking for a pilot," Sophia tells them, "you've got one."

Micah lets out a whoop of laughter and howls, "You serious, Soph? *You* can fly?"

She glares at him. Tartly, she snaps, "Yeah. I can. I've spent hundreds of hours in here the last two years. Figured someday I might wanna fly to Europe or Australia or somewhere else across the ocean."

"But that's a *video game*," counters Micah. "It can't be the same as flying an actual plane!"

"Real pilots train with it," she informs him. "Used to, anyway. Besides, if you want to get ahead of Lin Lai, I'm your best shot."

Sophia turns on her heel and fixes her fierce gaze on Ettore. "I know you didn't want to take me and Gabriel with you," she says. "But if you want to fly, you're gonna need me."

With one part disbelief, two parts amusement, Ettore stares back at her. He clearly admires her spunk and mettle. Even after coming within a literal inch of death, she is prepared to undergo unknown dangers to help them.

With the tone of someone happily conceding defeat, Ettore says, "I suppose we had better find ourselves a plane!"

SOPHIA THINKS SHE MIGHT throw up, and it has nothing to do with turbulence. It's the fact that she is operating a ten-passenger jet at twenty-eight thousand feet which has her feeling like she ate month-old tuna from the back of the fridge. Dario, sitting beside her in the cockpit, keeps casting leering glances her way. He's amused at her discomfort, which is made obvious by the sweat on her forehead and her jittery left leg.

Silently, Sophia prays the onboard navigation computers are working properly. The network of satellites known as the Global Positioning System—GPS—is still floating around space, alive and well and unaffected by humanity's disappearance. Without it, she knows they would have little hope of a successful flight to New York. Navigating roads with an atlas is one thing, but trying to fly a plane from Denver to the Big Apple would be impossible without the help of a working computer system.

"You were so confident when we were still on the ground," Dario comments. "Not so much now that you are in the air?"

"It's my first time. Cut me some slack," Sophia snaps back. She's irritated that Dario wanted to sit in the cockpit and learn how to fly, especially since all he does is criticize her.

Dario chuckles with dark amusement and says, "You know, they say taking off and cruising are the easy parts. But landing? That's when most accidents happen."

Sophia flashes him a look of pure disgust. "Are you seriously trying to freak me out right now? It sounds like you *want* me to crash. You're on this plane too, you know."

Dario laughs even harder. "Relax! I'm teasing. Of course I don't want that."

Sophia rolls her eyes and turns her attention to the various controls and gauges in front of her.

"Where did you get the scars?" Dario asks, staring and pointing at Sophia's left wrist.

Sophia reflexively tucks her hand beneath her butt to hide her wrist. "Nowhere," she replies.

Fortunately, Micah appears in the cockpit to save her from any further interrogation. Poking his head through the door, he says, "Kira made chicken. You want some? Can you eat while you're flying?"

Dario stands and says, "I could eat. The *girl* doesn't need me here anyway. Right?"

"Right," Sophia replies, ignoring Dario's belittling remark.

With one more derisive chuckle, the Spaniard leaves, and Micah slides into the vacant seat.

"Sorry 'bout Dario," he says, studying the control panel. "He's— you'll—well, who am I kidding? You ain't gonna warm up to him.

I've been with him a lot longer than you, and I'm about as warmed up as a popsicle in Antarctica."

His comment elicits a belly laugh from Sophia, and she asks, "Why is he even with you? Seems like he'd rather be alone."

"From what I heard," Micah explains, "he didn't really want to go with Ettore when they first bumped into each other. Genius that he is, our sly Italian convinced him. Good thing, too. Can't believe I just said that, but Dario is kind of a genius when it comes to machines. Cars, trains, boats, whatever. He can figure out pretty much anything that's got an engine."

A short silence follows. Sophia clears her throat and asks, "So, you came from South Carolina?"

"Mmm-hmm. Horse country," Micah answers. "I grew up workin' in stables for as long as I can remember. It was my dream to own my own horse ranch someday. But life doesn't usually work out the way we plan, I guess."

"No," Sophia agrees, chewing the inside of her lip. "I guess not. What was your family like?"

"It wasn't," Micah answers with a grim smile. In explanation of his vague answer, he continues. "My mom died of lung cancer when I was too young to remember. She was a pretty heavy smoker, from what I gather. And Dad got himself killed by a beer truck when I was nine. Rode bulls in the show for thirty years with hardly a scratch to show for it. Forgets to look both ways crossing the street, and he was gone, just like that." Micah snaps his fingers for emphasis.

"I'm so sorry," Sophia whispers. She feels awful for asking about his family.

Micah shrugs indifferently. He removes his black felt hat and stares down at it. "Dad bought me this a few months before he died, right after I won my first blue ribbon bull riding. He said it made me look like a real cowboy."

"What did you do after they were gone?" Sophia asks, hoping the question will lead to happier days on his timeline.

"My dad's brother took me in," says Micah. "Probably would've been better off on my own. He was a mean cuss. I worked my butt off in the stables, then on a pecan farm for a while, and that old thief took at least half of every paycheck for himself. 'To cover your room and board,' he'd say. More like lottery tickets and trips to the liquor store, I'd say."

"So why do you want to go back? What is there for you in 1978?"

A dreamy tenderness fills Micah's golden-brown eyes as he says, "This is gonna sound cliché, but ... there's a girl. Avonlea. I worked with her at the stables. We only knew each other a few months, but we were already plannin' a future together. We were gonna buy our own ranch, have a nice house, a few kids. And I'd never have to see that rotten uncle of mine again."

A flush of jealous warmth rises into Sophia's cheeks, and she realizes then that she might be harboring a tiny crush on Micah. Which is stupid, of course, because he's at least five years older than her—maybe more.

"And what about you?" he asks, jolting Sophia from her secret thoughts back to the conversation at hand.

"What do you mean?" Sophia says in response to his unclear question.

"Well, I know you're from Pennsylvania and that you've got a dog," Micah clarifies, "but what else should I know about Sophia Faraday?"

"I have a mom, dad, two brothers," she answers. She stares straight ahead, as if peering into past times. "I was playing hide-and-seek with my younger brother the day I slipped through time. He was counting, and I went and hid in the laundry closet under a pile of clothes. Bixby smelled me and followed me in there and wouldn't leave me alone, so I let him lie next to me. I waited and waited, but Eric—that's my little brother—never came.

"I eventually gave up and came out of the closet with Bixby. But everything was different. The furniture was moved around. There was dust all over everything. None of the lights would turn on. Then I walked into the dining room and saw the table covered with newspaper clippings—articles about a missing girl named Sophia Faraday. I figured it was some weird prank. I called out for my family, but no one answered. I watched out the front window for almost an hour, but I never saw even a single car drive by the house. I think that's when I knew something horrible happened. When I finally went to my older brother's room—his name's Darius—I looked at his atomic clock, and I saw that it wasn't 2021 anymore. It was 2026. November. More than five years *after* the day I'd been playing hide-and-seek."

"And one year after the rest of the world disappeared," Micah remarks.

"Yep," muses Sophia, using her fingernail to rub some dried gunk off one of the control panel knobs. "At least, that's what I guessed. All the latest newspapers I found had the same date: December 2, 2025."

"You ever wonder where they are? Where they went?" Micah asks. He tips his black hat so that it rests low over his eyes, then folds his hands on his belly. It almost looks like he wants to take a nap.

"Every day," Sophia answers.

From beneath his hat, Micah speaks timidly as he says, "You know, Soph, I didn't just come up here to shoot the breeze. I came to apologize."

"For what?"

"For the way I treated you and Gabe at first. I thought you were with the bad guys. I didn't really trust you 'til we got to your house, and I could see your story was true with my own eyes."

"It's okay," Sophia replies. "I have trust issues too. That's why Gabe and I didn't come right out and show ourselves to you. That's why we were sneaking around so much."

"You wanted to see what kind of people we were," Micah says matter-of-factly. "I get it."

He notices her discomfort and asks, "Something happen? That made you so suspicious?"

Sophia shrugs and says, "Yeah. I guess so."

"You don't have to talk about it if you don't want," Micah tells her, sensing her hesitation.

"No, it's just—I've never talked about it before now," stammers Sophia. She feels the walls around her heart crumbling, and she continues. "It happened eight months after my time slip. I was taking my first trip away from Pennsylvania—this was before I lived in Denver—and was driving around the Appalachian Mountains. When I was little, my mom and dad took me to the Biltmore, which is this huge mansion thing in Asheville."

"I've heard of it," Micah informs her.

"Anyway," she continues, "I wanted to go see it again, and I was just getting to Asheville when this old woman jumps out into the road and starts waving her arms. She was the first person I'd seen since playing hide-and-seek with my brother. I was so excited. Didn't really think about how bad people can be, and I let my guard down. Or never really put it up to begin with. I got out to talk to her, and she seemed really nice. Bixby didn't care for her, though. I guess I should have taken that as a warning.

"But I didn't. She said I was the first person she'd seen in a long time too, so she invited me to her house for dinner. It was just around the corner. Bixby was going a little nuts when I parked in front of her house, so I left him in the motorhome and went inside. As soon as I did, she ... *changed*. Started talking weird about how lonely she'd been. About how in this new world you can't let friends get away from you. But I didn't want to be rude, so I stuck around."

"Big mistake, I'm guessing," Micah comments. His hat is no longer hiding his eyes. He stares intently at Sophia as her story unfolds.

"Big mistake," she confirms. "While we were eating, she got up to refill my water. Next thing I knew, I was waking up in the basement, tied to a chair with a mega headache. She must have knocked me out when I wasn't looking."

"What did she do?" Micah asks, afraid to hear the answer.

"Nothing, really. Over the next couple days, she would come downstairs periodically to talk to me. I guess she really was just lonely. Totally psycho, but lonely."

"How'd you get away?"

Sophia says nothing at first. A series of images, each more horrifying than the last, parades up from her memory and in front of her eyes. She blinks them away, wills them to disappear, but they won't leave.

They never leave.

Finally, she utters three quiet words. "I killed her."

Chapter Twelve

THE PATH TO POWER

GRACEFUL FINGERS CARESS the book's ancient leather cover, like a mother stroking the face of her newborn baby. But for Lin Lai, this book is far more precious than any child ever could be.

It is a key. A key which unlocks not only the doors of Time, but of *power*.

And last night, for a few nauseating minutes, she thought she had lost it. She became careless, inattentive. Reveling in her victory, she forgot how quickly loyalty can turn to treachery, and she let her guard down.

She almost paid for her mistake with the Book of Relics itself. But Fate was kind to her, and the book was returned.

Now there is another who will pay.

The path to power is paved with many sacrifices. It seems like a lifetime ago that her father shared those words with her. At the time, she thought he sounded melodramatic.

She finally realizes just how true those words are.

A sudden, booming knock at the door disrupts her thoughts. She jumps with surprise, looking up from the book and into the mirror above the dresser.

"What is it?" she calls, annoyed at the interruption.

"I gathered everyone, as you requested," replies a powerful male voice with a thick Scottish accent. "We're outside in the parking lot. Blue is there too."

Lin notes his hesitancy in speaking that final sentence.

Sometimes loyalty is earned with love. Other times it must be coerced through fear. Today is a day for the latter.

"Good," she says. "I will be there in one minute."

Lin opens the top drawer of the motel dresser and gingerly places the Book of Relics inside. She covers it with a folded white sheet, then shuts the drawer to conceal her treasure. Although she won't be apart from it long, she wants to be sure it is hidden from searching eyes and protected from greedy hands.

Before turning away from the mirror, she notices what she is wearing. Khaki hiking shorts and a bright blue tank top aren't exactly the image of ruthlessness she would like to project, but they'll have to do. There is no time to change right now.

As she reaches for the sleek, black bow and arrow-stocked quiver lying on her queen-size bed, she detects a tremor in her slender hands. She pauses. Closes her eyes. Sucks in a deep breath. Holds it for three seconds, then blows it out loudly. As she does, she envisions herself exhaling her own weakness. Twice more she does this before reopening her eyes.

The moment of hesitation is over. When she reaches for her bow again, her hands are steady with resolve.

After all, she didn't become her university's top archer by doubting herself.

Lin slings the quiver onto her back, then adjusts it to the perfect position. She must be able to reach back and grab its many razor-sharp arrows with ease. Gripping the bow in her left hand, she adopts an archer's pose. She draws the bowstring, ensuring that it has proper tension and is in working order.

All is exactly as it should be.

Lin approaches her motel room's door and stops there. She takes one more deep, relaxing breath, then opens it and steps outside.

It is scarcely midmorning, but central Indiana's heat and humidity are already building. She and her attendants have wasted too much of the day. They should be on the road, traveling eastward, putting as much distance as possible between themselves and any potential pursuers.

She must make quick work of the task at hand.

Of the *traitor* at hand.

Lin peers down from the second-floor walkway. A handful of people have assembled upon the blacktop below. Seven pairs of eyes stare up at her, expectant and anxious.

One pair does not.

Lin takes the cement-slab staircase down to ground level. As she descends, she takes careful stock of her nervous crew.

Attendants, she reminds herself. They are subordinates. Not equals.

Never equals.

There is the gangly, pale, and grim-faced Stoker, her medic. The stocky British-Asian fellow next to him is simply called Q. He's her technology and equipment expert. Mouse, with his quick and beady eyes, has no area of specialty other than following orders efficiently and with a doglike desire to please. The plump woman beside him, who goes by the name Caesar, also oversees many of the group's odds and ends, but with a special emphasis on mealtime duties. Cook and

Columbia, two women who are total opposites in every way but one, are the group's navigation and transportation specialists.

Of course, there is also Redbeard. He's the one who knocked on her motel door. The Scottish special forces soldier has served as her right-hand man for over a year. Among all her attendants, his is the only opinion she truly respects when it comes to strategy and planning. While she regards the others as useful in their own ways, she views Redbeard as an invaluable asset in the pursuit of her goals.

Finally, Lin's eyes rest upon the woman kneeling in the middle of the group. Her hands and feet are bound behind her, mouth gagged with an old strip of cloth. Terror fills her emerald-green eyes. As she watches Lin Lai descend the stairs, her entire body quakes with fear.

"Good morning, Blue," Lin says, her voice too sickly sweet to be genuine. Approaching the captive woman, she clucks her tongue like a mother scolding a child. "My, you look terrible. Trouble sleeping last night?"

Blue doesn't make a sound. She stares forward, desperately avoiding eye contact.

"My apologies," says Lin. She crouches and unties Blue's gag. "It must be impossible to answer with this in your mouth. Now, what do you have to say for yourself?"

"It—it wasn't what you think," Blue stammers. Her lofty British accent doesn't sound so noble with its fearful quiver. "I wasn't trying to steal the book. I was just curious. Wanted a peek inside, that's all."

"Ah, so this was all just a misunderstanding!" Lin exclaims.

"Just a misunderstanding," confirms Blue.

"Then Redbeard and Columbia were simply ... *misunderstanding* when they caught you preparing to drive off in one of my vehicles? And when I searched your backpack, it was my *misunderstanding* that I found the Book of Relics inside? Was that some other ancient book dedicated to the pieces of a different time machine? And was I *misunderstanding* your intentions to find the relics without us? To steal all *my* power for yourself?"

Blue lowers her eyes but says nothing.

Like a snake striking its prey, Lin seizes Blue's jaw and forces her chin upward.

"Look at me when I speak to you!" she hisses, also *sounding* like an angry snake. "I do not care that you were once some British baroness, and I do not care what kings or queens you once dined with. In my new world, you are whoever and whatever I decide. And I say you are a worm."

Blue's shuddering intensifies. Frightened tears drip from her cheeks onto the blacktop below.

"Please," she whispers, struggling to find her voice. "Please, don't hurt me. I will never disobey or betray you again. I promise. I will be loyal to you every hour—every *second*—of my life. I swear it!"

Lin lets go of Blue's face. She feels another flutter of hesitation's wings beating inside her stomach. As in the motel room, she closes her eyes and takes a deep breath.

When she opens them again, she looks at Redbeard and says, "Cut her ropes."

Redbeard appears surprised at the command, but also relieved. He unsheathes a long knife from his belt and kneels beside Blue. It doesn't take the sharp blade long to slice through her bonds.

Blue is now weeping tears of joy. Through her blubbering, she repeats the words "thank you" at least a dozen times.

"Stand up," Lin orders.

Blue does.

Seizing a shoulder, Lin spins Blue until she is facing the opposite direction. Across the motel parking lot is a line of trees which marks the edge of a forest.

"You served me well for a time," says Lin, "but the hour of your usefulness is past. I can no longer trust you, so here we must part ways. Forever."

"No," begs Blue. "Please, don't send me away. I don't want to be alone again. Please!"

"My judgment is decided, and it will not be undone," says Lin. She points to the forest beyond the parking lot. "See those trees? You will enter them, and you will not return. I never want to see your traitor's face again. Do you understand?"

Blue seems to realize that no amount of pleading will reverse her fate. Wiping the tears from her cheeks, she nods solemnly.

"Then good luck," whispers Lin. "And goodbye."

Blue doesn't run, but she does make quickly for the trees. She realizes, perhaps, that she caught Lin Lai in a rare moment of mercy and doesn't want to press her good fortune.

Lin turns toward rest of her people. They appear relieved. While they didn't condone Blue's traitorous actions, they also had no desire to see her punished too severely.

It is a weakness Lin cannot allow. Not within herself. Not among her people.

Like a cracked whip, she doubles back to face Blue again. The traitor has almost arrived within the safety of the trees.

In one fluid motion, Lin raises her bow, notches an arrow, and lets it fly. Before anyone can raise a cry of surprise or protest, her bow-string hums again as she sends a second arrow on its way.

Blue doesn't make a sound as her body crumples into the long grass.

"Now I can be certain we have parted ways forever," Lin says, making sure she speaks loudly enough for all her attendants to hear. She turns to find their faces painted with shock and fear.

Her gaze shifts deliberately from one to the other as she addresses them. "Remember the oaths of loyalty you swore to me, and do not forget them. If you do, there is no amount of luck which will rescue you from my wrath. Are there any *misunderstandings?* Or have I made myself clear?"

Seven heads nod, and seven pairs of lips mumble their understanding.

"Good," says Lin. "Follow me, and you will not only *see* great things. You will *become* them. But make no mistake. There may be many princes and princesses in the new world I will make, but there can only be one Empress of Time."

Like an immediate challenge to Lin Lai's declarations, the faint drone of an engine draws her attention upward. There, sailing miles above them across the sky, is a small jet.

Her jaw drops, and a new rage boils within her. She snarls his name, once so loved, now so loathed.

"*Ettore.*"

The rest of her attendants exchange alarmed glances. Then every eye turns to Lin for instructions, a hive of bees looking as one to their queen.

Pointing at Mouse and Caesar, Lin says, "Bury her quickly. The rest of you, pack your things. As soon as Blue is in the ground, we leave."

Lin hurries to her motel room. She barely makes it to the bathroom toilet before she throws up. Afterward, she allows herself a single minute to cry.

Blue is the first person she has ever killed.

When Lin is done, she wipes her eyes, rinses her mouth, and washes her face. She stares at herself in the bathroom mirror. Except for the blue tank top, she again appears hard and merciless.

She prays it will be easier next time. Because she knows there will be a "next time."

Once more, she hears her father's clear voice in her ears.

The path to power is paved with many sacrifices.

Lin Lai has now laid her first brick upon that path. And, if her father's words are indeed true, many more will follow.

Chapter Thirteen

TRANSATLANTIC

MICAH STARES AHEAD through the airplane's windscreen. He appears unshocked by Sophia's bloody revelation about the old woman in Asheville. Finally, he says, "I guess we have that in common. Killing someone, you know? But you've gotta do what you've gotta do to survive in this crazy world."

Sophia doesn't reply. She wants the conversation to be over.

Micah senses her discomfort, so he changes the subject. "It sure looks stormy up there."

Sophia has been so immersed in her story that she failed to notice what lay ahead. Like an army of black-bellied anvils, a line of thunderstorms guards the horizon.

"We headin' into those?" Micah asks with a note of concern.

Sophia nods, then turns her attention to the control panel. She immediately begins dropping altitude and says, "Would you tell the others to buckle up? This might get bumpy." As Micah jumps up to follow orders, she adds, "And send Dario up here. I might need another set of hands."

Moments later, the Spaniard is back in the copilot's chair. With a smug grin he says, "Can't handle it yourself?"

Sophia is too concerned to take the bait. "We're only a couple hundred miles from New York City, but we're going to switch to Newark. It's across the bay in New Jersey. Anyway, it's a lot more open. We'll have better visibility as we land, and we won't have to worry about smashing into any skyscrapers."

"So? What do you need me to do?" Dario asks impatiently.

"I need another pair of eyes," Sophia answers. "If the runway looks like it's crumbling or breaking apart, or if it's blocked with other planes, I need you to tell me so we can take a different approach. I could use your help with a few other things too. The plane's GPS *should* know exactly where the runway is, and the nav system *should* do most of the work landing it. But I'm gonna be busy stabilizing us and staying ready for a manual takeover, especially if we're in the middle of one of those storms, so I might need you to work some of the controls. Got it?"

For once, Dario doesn't offer a sniping remark. He even appears impressed by Sophia's command of the situation as he says, "Got it. *Boss.*"

The moment the words escape his lips, a downdraft churned by the impending storm punches the jet, and it lurches violently. Shouts erupt from the plane's cabin, but Sophia and Dario ignore them.

The rookie pilot prays that the plane remains in one piece. Nobody has serviced this airborne hunk of steel and fiberglass for almost four years. Sophia knows all it takes is one wobbly rivet, one weakened flap, and their flight would end up a glowing lump of molten metal in a field.

They descend within three thousand feet of the ground, and rain splatters the windscreen. They are passing beneath the swollen stomach of an especially gluttonous thundercloud, but apart from a few shudders of turbulence, the trip remains uneventful.

Sophia takes the plane for a low-level lap above the Newark runways. She tilts the metal bird to allow Dario a good look at the ground.

"Is it clear? The runway?" she asks.

"There are a few abandoned planes, but it's mostly clear," Dario answers. His voice is devoid of its usual snark. Then he asks, "Can you land in this much rain?"

Sophia shrugs and answers, "I've only done it on the simulator. But yeah, I should be able to. In theory. Besides, I don't have much choice. There isn't enough fuel left to fly around looking for a dry runway." She thinks for a moment, then adds, "I'm gonna bring us back around. You make sure we're coming in on a clear runway."

"I'll do my best," says Dario, "but it might be difficult with the rain."

Sophia wonders if anyone her age has ever tried landing a jet before now. The idea makes her strangely proud, and with the pride comes a shot of confidence.

She directs the jet in a wide arc, until they are approaching one long runway head on. To the east she sees the Statue of Liberty standing tall in her cloak of mist. Fog shrouds the rest of New York City. Only the faintest shadows of Manhattan's mighty skyscrapers look down on the Hudson River and the Upper Bay.

"Is it clear?" she asks Dario. The confidence drains from her suddenly, replaced by wild nerves.

"The runway is partially blocked on the left side," Dario answers, "but we should have plenty of room to avoid it. I think."

Sophia spots the commercial jetliner. Once upon a time, it had been turning onto the runway before it died and stalled forever.

"I see it," she confirms. "I'll steer clear."

To the folks sitting in the cabin, Dario yells, "Grab on to something! We're about to land!"

The wheels touch down with a screech. Sophia curses loudly as the jet heaves upward again, like someone stepping barefooted on hot pavement. Moments later, the tires hit the tarmac a second time and remain there. The rest of the jet, however, convulses violently back and forth, as if they have landed in the sea and are caught in great waves.

Sophia realizes her mistake too late. She underestimated how soon after touchdown they would reach the commercial jet. At the last possible moment, she jerks the sticks wildly to one side, but instead of steering the aircraft away from the obstacle, she sends it into a full spin. From somewhere far behind them—Or was it in front? They're spinning too fast to know—she hears the awful shriek of twisting, tearing metal as the two planes make contact.

Sophia is certain she's killed them all.

Then, as quickly as the chaos began, it's over. Everything is silent—except for the choked gurgle from Sophia's own throat as she vomits between her legs and onto the floor.

"You alright?" asks Dario. He, too, looks a bit green in the gills.

"Yeah," Sophia replies, before heaving up more of her breakfast. "Go check on everyone else. Get them off the plane."

She knows they might still be in danger. If anything has caught fire, an explosion could follow at any moment. The rain will be cold, but at least it won't kill them.

To her immense relief, no one is seriously injured. Micah has a small cut on his forehead from a shattered lightbulb, and each of the twins sports a lump near her temple due to a colliding of their skulls. Other than those minor injuries, her passengers are fine.

Two minutes later, Sophia is outside, carrying her hiking backpack through the rain. She sees that a sizeable chunk of the tail came off during their collision with the other plane. If the impact had come near the middle or front, the casualties certainly would have been far worse.

She can't stop shaking, and she knows it has little to do with the downpour. She was so cocky about her ability to fly. Her overwhelming desire to accompany Ettore overrode the logical part of her brain, and the mistake nearly cost her life and the lives of six others— plus Bixby. The serious nature of this relic hunt hits her suddenly, and she finds herself in the grips of a powerful desire to return home to her chickens, her electricity, her queen bed, and her flight simulator.

Video games don't kill you when you crash, she tells herself.

The storm-soaked crew hikes a half-mile across the airport's concrete fields before arriving at the terminal. Inside, everybody changes into the driest clothes they have. They are soon huddled together, facing each other on two rows of black airport seats.

"So," Kira asks, addressing Ettore, "what's next?"

The short Italian ponders their options, then says, "Unless anyone wants to attempt a transatlantic plane trip, it would seem most reasonable that we travel by boat now."

Dario scowls darkly at this idea but doesn't speak a word in objection.

"Trains, planes, boats," mutters Micah. "All kinds of firsts for me on this adventure! Cars and horses—that's all it ever was for me 'til now."

Kylah clears her throat and says, "I don't know much about boats and sailing, but won't that be a little dangerous once we're up in the Arctic waters around Norway? I mean, this won't exactly be like taking a motorboat around the lake."

"What other choice do we have?" Ettore replies.

"She's right," Dario says softly. His arms are crossed, his expression dour. "The sea at those latitudes becomes increasingly treacherous. Very unpredictable. But clearly"—He glances meaningfully at Sophia—"taking an airplane is out of the question."

Sophia shrinks in her seat. She's glad the cold rain has already turned her cheeks pink. She doesn't want the others to notice her blushing with shame.

"Here's what I think," Dario goes on, leaning forward and lacing his fingers together. "If we're going to cross the ocean, it has to be by boat. So, we find a boat. But instead of sailing all the way to the North Cape, we'll cut through the English Channel between Great Britain and France, then head up and across to Norway. The North Sea isn't always the tamest, but we'll find more cover between England and Scandinavia than we would in the open waters of the Arctic Ocean. Once we arrive at the southern shore of Norway, we can find other means of transportation for the rest of the journey."

Ettore casts Dario a hard, calculating look and says, "It appears Dario has thought this through. Let's find some food and get some rest. First thing tomorrow, we trade our plane for a ship."

LIKE AIR LET OUT OF A TIRE, everything in Sophia's lungs rushes out with a hissing gasp as her back hits the sun-scorched deck. Her attacker, standing over her in victory, extends a hand to help her to her feet.

"Okay, what did you do wrong that time?" Kylah asks, once Sophia has regained her breath.

"I overcommitted to the block on my right side and exposed myself too much on the left," Sophia answers. "Right?"

"That was part of it," says Kylah. "You're also letting your eyes wander too much."

Sophia nods her understanding. For the past six days, ever since the company set to sea from the Hudson River Yacht Club, she's been killing boredom by studying the art of kickboxing. Kylah and Kira, she's learned, used to co-own a studio in Charleston, and they've been taking turns training her. Although both have assured her that she's a quick student, Sophia feels like more of a failure every time she crashes onto the deck.

Kylah senses her frustration and says, "I think that's enough for now."

After grabbing a bottled water from the beverage fridge, Sophia collapses onto a cushioned seat next to Gabriel. He's been playing a neck-and-neck match of Uno against Kira, who swiped the card game from one of the airport shops in Newark. Here on the yacht's covered deck, they can enjoy the refreshing sea breeze and escape the sun's harsh rays at the same time. Somewhere above them, Dario is piloting the ship toward England and, eventually, the southern coast of Norway. The other two men could be anywhere among the luxury yacht's three decks. The *Seas All That* has no shortage of rooms where they might be hiding.

"Uno!" Gabriel exclaims, slapping his second-to-last card down on table.

Kira responds with an overdramatic "Uh-oh!" before using one of her own cards to change the playable color from blue to yellow.

"Yes!" the nine-year-old cries triumphantly. "That's the one I needed!"

He plays his final card. Exuberant in victory, he pumps both fists high into the air.

Sophia smiles. It's nice to see Gabriel enjoying himself so much.

Bixby, who has been seasick the entire voyage, raises his head from the boy's lap. Unable to see what all the excitement is about, he lowers it again and closes his miserable eyes.

Kira chuckles softly and says, "You know, this is my daughter Tonya's favorite game. She's really good at it too!"

"Yeah?" Gabriel replies. "What was Regina's favorite?"

"Oh, she doesn't like card games very much," Kira says, answering the question about her other twin daughter. "She likes pretending and using her imagination to play."

Sophia closes her eyes. She can't help but feel thankful for Kira. Over the past few days, the older woman has become something of a role model for her. Kira is strong and tough—she has mastered several forms of martial arts besides kickboxing—but she's also kind and caring. She spends almost all her time playing games with Gabriel, or nursing seasick Ettore, or applying aloe to the sunburnt passengers of the *Seas All That*. In a way, Kira reminds Sophia of her own mother. Both women live with dedication for the people they love and a determination to keep them happy and safe—although Maria Faraday wouldn't have been quite as handy in a fight.

Kylah plunks down next to Sophia. She wipes beads of sweat from her brow and takes a long drink from her water bottle. After a few deep breaths she says, "Do you know what your main problem is, Soph? With the kickboxing?"

The girl looks away, embarrassed, and asks, "What?"

"You get in your own head too much."

"What do you mean?" Sophia can't help but feel a little insulted.

"You're thinking too much about making the *wrong* move," Kylah explains. "It slows your reactions and messes up your judgment. Just think about making the *right* move. Then you won't clutter your mind with a bunch of unnecessary possibilities that aren't useful anyway. You'll be able to act quicker."

Sophia nods thoughtfully. Secretly, though, she decides she'll just use the pistol if they run into trouble. *Much* more effective than kicking someone.

The conversation is interrupted moments later by Micah. He appears giddy with excitement as he bellows, "Land ho!"

Everyone hurries to the bow. Sure enough, a hazy but solid point of land is barely visible on the horizon.

"Dario thinks it's England," says Micah. "If he's right, we'll be able to get off this boat and spend the night onshore."

Sophia feels unexpectedly nervous. She thought she would enjoy a break from the boat, but now that they are nearing the next leg of their journey, she wonders what fresh dangers will arrive with it.

She shakes her head and pushes back against the fears. She can't let herself dwell on them, because they cannot help her. Nor can she focus too much on the goal. The end is too distant. If that's where she sets her sights, she'll only find herself overwhelmed at what it will take to get there.

Instead, she must focus on the journey. The adventure of a lifetime. She will give everything she can to help find the lost relics of the Antikythera Device. She will marvel at the wonders of the world that she sees along the way.

Above all, she will enjoy the rebirth of friendship—of *family*—which has graced her young life once more.

Chapter Fourteen

THE WATERS AND ROADS
OF NORWAY

"THE WHITE CLIFFS OF DOVER!" Ettore exclaims. He is staring north across the crystalline waters of the English Channel. In the distance is a line of sheer, white chalk cliffs.

To Sophia, these White Cliffs of Dover resemble a row of well-cleaned teeth left by some giant of an ancient age. Sure, they have a ruggedly serene sort of beauty, but they don't compare to a thousand natural landmarks she has seen in the States.

Ettore views them differently. A childlike grin overtakes him as he muses, "I haven't seen them since I was a boy, when my parents took me to England on holiday. Of course, that was after the War."

"What war?" asks Gabriel quizzically.

"The Great War," Ettore clarifies. "It was the only time in my life I remember the world truly at peace. Except for now, I suppose."

The *Seas All That* and her passengers are on day seven of their journey. After spending the previous night in the port town of Salcombe, they continued their trip eastward between Great Britain and the north coast of France.

After nearly a week of nothing but open water, Sophia is glad to see land again. Especially land as beautiful as this!

Dario believes they should reach Oslo, situated on the southern coast of Norway, sometime tomorrow. From there they will drive north through both Norway and Sweden. With any luck, they'll arrive at *Promontorium Boreale*—the "North Cape"—and the first piece of the Antikythera Device within three days' time.

"Well," says Kira, elbowing Sophia playfully, "do you plan to gawk at the landscape all day? Or should we have a lesson?"

Truthfully, Sophia would rather gawk, but because she doesn't want to disappoint Kira, she says, "We could do a lesson."

As always, they head to the open area of the yacht's aft deck. As she warms up and stretches, Sophia casually scans the watery horizon behind the boat. There are seabirds floating on the breeze, scouting for shallow fish. High above, whiffs of white cloud decorate the sapphire sky.

She freezes, squinting. Surely her eyes are playing a trick! Like a lone pencil mark on a piece of blue construction paper, a black speck intrudes upon the sea and sky behind them.

She grabs Kira's arm and points to the dark spot.

Kira tenses immediately, then yells, "Ettore! Micah! Everyone! Someone's following us!"

In moments, the lazy yacht becomes a flurry of excitement as everyone rushes to join them on the stern.

As soon as Ettore spots the pursuing ship, he says, "We must meet upstairs with Dario."

A minute later, everyone is gathered in the wood-paneled steering room.

"It has to be Lin," Dario declares upon hearing the news. He spits the words hatefully and follows them with a curse. "I thought we had a bigger head start."

"As did I," Ettore agrees.

"So? What's that mean for us?" Micah asks.

"Nothing," Dario replies. "We stick to the plan."

Ettore gazes thoughtfully at the Spaniard. Sophia can see the gears and screws turning in the physicist's head as he considers the situation.

"I think the plan must change," he announces.

Dario frowns. He looks like he knew Ettore would say that.

"Change to what?" Kylah asks, glancing around the room. "Go after a different relic instead?"

"No," replies Ettore, "not that."

"He wants to keep sailing north," Dario explains, reading Ettore's mind. "The roads through Sweden are winding and forested. If there are downed trees blocking the road, we might lose hours trying to find a way around them. If we stick to the sea, Ettore knows we could save a lot of time. *Potentially.*"

"Potentially?" says Kylah. "What do you mean?"

"*If* the weather holds out, *if* we have favorable winds, *if* the seas aren't too rough," lists Dario. "We need many variables to go our way. The seas north of here can be very dangerous. Even deadly."

Sophia is surprised at Dario's intuition. Her first impressions of him were of a rash and reckless scoundrel. Now she is beginning to see that he can be both thoughtful and calculated.

"If Lin notices us steering toward Oslo, she'll know she might gain an advantage by taking the sea," Ettore says ponderously. "If she sees us sailing northward, she'll know she can't give up the chase. Either way, I believe she will travel by sea. If we want to be certain we're still ahead of her, it means we must do the same."

Dario curses, then says, "I know you're right, but it's risky."

"It will be the same risk she is taking," Ettore replies.

"It'll be a miracle if we don't all end up dead," Dario murmurs, deep in thought. "Are we sure the risk is worth the reward?"

"I will force no one to go any further than they want," Ettore says, glancing around at the rest of his crew. "Say the word, and we will find the nearest port. You may go on your way."

Everyone remains silent, though there are a few nervous glances from person to person.

It's Micah who breaks the silence. "We're with ya, Ettie. I don't question your decisions."

Dario shrugs and says, "Then it seems like we're sailing north. I will spend some time with the maps and charts to find a good place for making landfall. Plus a few backups in case the sea and weather turn on us."

"Good," says Ettore, before addressing the rest. "We are fast approaching the location of the first relic. So is Lin. If all goes well, we will beat her to the location, but not by much. Because Lin has the Book of Relics, she holds a huge advantage over us, as you all know. This means we must use every other tool to *our* advantage, so that we can find the relic as quickly as possible."

"And how are we supposed to do that? We don't even know what it looks like!" Kylah exclaims with a touch of exasperation.

The physicist snatches a yellow legal pad and pen from the short end table next to him. Slowly, he writes something on it. When he's finished, he says, "It is true. We do not know what the relic looks like. Nor do we have the book's clues to pinpoint its exact location when we arrive at the North Cape. Now is the time for me to share with you what I *do* know."

He flips the yellow pad around so everyone can see it. Written on it are ten letters. Some are familiar, but others look strange. It reads:

ΑΝΤΙΚΥΘΗΡΑ

"An-tick-yoo—what's it mean?" asks a perplexed Micah.

"They are the Greek letters which spell out the word *Antikythera,*" Ettore answers. "According to one of the books I found in the Vatican, the locations of the Hallowed Vaults are all marked with one of these letters. Find the letter, find the Vault. Understand?"

"And ... that's it? That's all we've got to help us find it?" Kira asks. There's no mistaking her skepticism.

"More or less, yes," the Italian replies apologetically. "I know it is not much, but unless we obtain the Book of Relics, or I find other clues in my books, this is all we have."

Dario grunts his disapproval and mutters, "All we have is nothing."

Micah approaches the problem with his usual brand of dry humor. "No problem. Like tryin' to find a needle in a haystack. But with a blindfold on to make it harder."

"Yes, that is the game," Ettore admits. "Please make sure your belongings are packed and ready to leave at a moment's notice. With Lin so close behind us, we truly have no time to spare. The race is on, and we cannot lose."

The crew disperses.

Belowdecks, in her luxurious stateroom, Sophia stuffs her blue hiking backpack full of clothes, toiletries, and other belongings. Then she returns to the deck, where Kira is waiting to begin their kickboxing training session. They're halfway through when Dario announces the plan to dock at a tiny village named Skarsvåg. This will bring them as close to the North Cape as possible before they will be forced to drive.

As he leaves, his grumbles reiterate that he thinks it's a longshot, and that they'll all probably die trying to get there.

By evening, the coastal mountains of southeast Norway stand majestic and proud on the starboard horizon. They glow bronze and orange, as if the sinking sun has turned them into molten rock. Below the higher slopes, pine-forested islands and seaside hills create a skirt of deep green.

Sophia thinks she can smell the rich earth and fragrant trees carried on the salty breeze. She wishes they had time to go ashore. How she would love to explore those forests and fjords and quaint seaside villages!

Another day, she tells herself. For now, they must keep ahead of the boat following them. Lin Lai won't stop to smell the pines. Neither can she.

Sophia glances backward at the black smudge on the southern horizon, and a sense of uneasiness shivers down her spine. She could be wrong, but she thinks it's getting bigger.

Night falls, and with it a million stars salt the sky. Everything else is inky blackness in the moonless world.

For a short while, Sophia sits on the aft deck. Kira and Kylah keep her company, talking about the old world, their families and friends and homes. Eventually, the chill becomes too much for Sophia, and she crawls into her bed for what she knows might be her last comfortable sleep in a while.

When she awakens hours later, the sea has changed. She feels the difference immediately. The up-and-down conveyor belt of swells is more dramatic than before. Looking out the window, she sees it is still dark. She dresses hurriedly. Without leaving the warmth of the boat's insides, she climbs the spiral staircase into the steering room.

She expected to find only Dario here. She is happy to learn that Ettore is with him.

"Good morning," the Italian greets her warmly. His face is pale, his eyes sunken. His seasickness must be even worse than before.

"What are you doing awake?" he asks.

"Couldn't sleep," she answers. "Are the waves getting bigger? Or is it just my imagination?"

"Bigger and meaner," says Dario. His eyes are locked on the sea outside. "And coming straight out of the north."

It is then that Sophia notices the stars are gone. Clouds have erased them from the night sky.

"We may have to cut our voyage short," Ettore informs her. "We will see whether or not this storm passes."

It doesn't. As the black morning turns to a murky gray, the swells grow larger and the wind fiercer. Dario reassures the rest, telling them the yacht was built to handle this kind of rough weather. At the same time, he admits that if it becomes any worse, they'll have no choice but to go ashore.

Early morning turns to late morning, and late morning into afternoon. The situation doesn't worsen, but it also doesn't improve. Gabriel soon joins Bixby and Ettore in the seasick club, and Kira finds her hands full caring for both dog and boy. By midafternoon, each has vomited at least a half-dozen times.

Around four o'clock, the strong headwind becomes an all-out gale. Dario and Ettore, who haven't left the steering room once, decide to make for the port town of Narvik, a village nestled east of them at the crook of a deep bay. To the north, a crescent-shaped set of islands gives them some cover from the winds, and before long the swells shrink to half their former size.

Icy rain is spattering the yacht when Dario maneuvers it into Narvik's harbor. Although no one has seen Lin's boat since nightfall, the company wastes no time finding a pair of vehicles. The three men select a black Volvo, while the twins pile into a tiny blue Skoda with Sophia, Gabriel, and Bixby. Within minutes, the two-car caravan begins its long journey northeast toward the roof of Europe.

And the relic awaiting them there.

With Bixby's warm head against her stomach, Sophia immediately falls asleep in the back seat.

Darkness has fallen by the time she awakens. She realizes they must have stopped at least once, because Kira has replaced Kylah as their driver. Rain soaks the windshield, and the years-old wipers are doing a terrible job clearing it away. Wind buffets the car, causing it to shiver and shake. Ahead, winding through the mountainous terrain, are the Volvo's red taillights.

"How long do we have to drive?" the girl asks wearily.

The voice startles Kira, and she jumps in her seat. Realizing it was the newly awakened Sophia who asked the question, she rubs her bleary eyes and replies, "Not sure. It's hard to tell. These roads wind in and out of dozens of fjords along the seacoast. Plus, this weather isn't helping. Soooo, half a day? Maybe more?"

A spiderweb of lighting rips open the sky. The tremendous peal of accompanying thunder awakens Bixby, and the boxer mutt looks up at Sophia for reassurance. She responds by pulling his head close to her stomach. This comforts the dog, and he closes his eyes again.

On and on through the wild night they drive. When both vehicles are low on gas, they stop in a tiny seaside town and trade for two different ones. After a quick look at an atlas stolen from the Volvo, Dario determines they are less than halfway to the North Cape. The news is disheartening for everyone but Ettore, whose eyes remain lit with a fierce gleam of determination.

"We must still be ahead of Lin," he says. "This weather will have slowed her progress too."

Dawn is breaking when they stop to swap vehicles again. Now they are in Alta, which seems a bit larger than the other towns they've passed. They luck out at a gas station, finding two vehicles whose

tanks had been filled moments before their owners disappeared forever. When they switch cars, the wind is so violent and the rain so
torrential that after only a few seconds outside, everyone is drenched.
Sophia wishes with all her heart she would have grabbed some dry
clothes to change into, especially after learning the new car's heater is
broken.

Past Alta, the road finally breaks free of the winding seacoast, and
they travel up into higher country. At first Sophia is happy for the
change. The brightening daylight, however, reveals the true terror of
the storm. Many of the small, scrubby plants carpeting the high heath
are being ripped up by the roots and flung across the roadway. Whenever they pass below any hill, Sophia cringes as the gale hurls sand and
pebbles against her window.

With a white-knuckled grip, Kira locks both hands onto the steering wheel. Sitting in the passenger seat, Kylah clutches her armrests
for dear life.

Sophia is glad when they descend toward the coast again, but only
for a moment. Then she realizes that if the car loses the road here, it
will mean plummeting a hundred feet down jagged rocks into the
frigid waters of the Arctic Ocean below. She gulps and hopes Ettore,
driving the car ahead of them, will slow down some.

They at last receive a break from the weather when they enter a
cavernous tunnel. For a long time they travel downhill, until Sophia
is quite certain they are, in fact, beneath the sea itself. A few miles later,
the road turns upward again.

Just before arriving at the tunnel's exit, the men's red Audi
screeches to a halt. Micah jumps out and jogs toward them.

Kira stops too. She rolls down her window and asks, "What's going
on? Everything alright?"

"Fine," Micah replies, his voice echoing around the cavern walls.

"When we get outta the tunnel, keep driving a little way and then pull over. Dario—God bless him—might've had the best idea of his life."

"What is it?" Kira inquires suspiciously.

"You'll see!" Micah calls over his shoulder as he hustles back to the Audi.

Though she doesn't know the plan, Kira does as asked. Outside the tunnel, again within the jaws of the savage storm, she pulls to the side of the road. Without a care for the deluge, she rolls down her window and looks back to learn what kind of scheme the men have concocted.

For a few minutes, the Audi remains parked at the tunnel's mouth. Then Dario hops out. Carrying a bulky backpack around his shoulders, he hurries into the tunnel and is swallowed up by its darkness. One minute passes, then two. Still, Dario does not return. Finally, around the four-minute mark, he reemerges, running at a full sprint.

Sophia realizes he is no longer carrying the backpack.

Dario dives into the car. Ettore speeds forward, driving like someone fleeing a horde of savage monsters.

Then the ground beneath them shudders, and Sophia wonders if they have been caught in an earthquake. A tremendous roar bellows forth from the mouth of the cave, followed by a rush of dust and stone, as the tunnel vomits up its insides.

The tremors stop as quickly as they started. The rain and ripping winds are again the only sounds Sophia hears.

It takes a moment for her to realize what has happened. When she does, she can't keep herself from laughing.

Ettore stops his car beside theirs. Dario, sitting in the passenger seat, rolls down his window. His face beams with a wickedly satisfied grin as he says, "I've always wanted to blow something up. Let's see Lin follow us through *that*."

Chapter Fifteen

PROMONTORIUM BOREALE

TIRED, HUNGRY, AND DAMP, the gang reaches Europe's northernmost point shortly before noon. The storm's anger is now so savage, it looks more like nighttime outside than midday.

Their little vehicles wobble under hurricane-force winds when they park in front of the North Cape Hall. The low, broad building looks quite out of place among the windswept Arctic hills. Stone and mortar make up the visitor center's front façade. Behind this there is a modern rotunda topped with a large white sphere, which looks like the pompom on a giant winter cap.

"Remember," says Kira, staring intensely out the rain-streaked windshield, "there will most likely be another Immovable inside. Take whatever you need to protect yourself."

Sophia gives her a halfhearted thumbs-up. Now that they've arrived, she isn't so sure she wants to go through with the plan.

But it's too late to back out, and she knows it. Once more, she pats her hip. The pistol is right where it should be, secure and loaded. She prays she won't have to use it, but somehow it feels inevitable. Before long she will have more blood on her hands. Maybe not today. Maybe not tomorrow. But eventually.

When they exit the safety and warmth of the car, Sophia's body heat is sucked away instantly. The waterproof windbreaker is no match for the icy downpour driven by the cyclone's winds.

Seven people and one dog hurry from two cars. In front of the main entrance, they huddle together.

Over the din of the storm, Ettore shouts, "The moment we step inside these doors, you must stay alert. Danger may come at any moment. Keep your ears and eyes open and your guard up."

Dario fingers the long knife strapped to his belt and responds, "No need to worry about me!" He seems excited that he might get to use it.

Looks of disgust cross the twins' faces, but they say nothing.

Micah yanks hard on one of the doors, as though he might have to rip it off its hinges, but it opens easily. Everybody shuffles inside and into a low, narrow entryway. Beyond this, the North Cape Hall opens into a cavernous room with a lofty ceiling. Floor-to-ceiling windows on the building's north end reveal a hundred yards of barren rock beyond. After this, a drop into the sea. Near the cliff's edge stands a monument of sorts. It is like a globe—or, rather, the skeleton of a globe—made of black steel bars and raised high on a pedestal.

"We will begin our search indoors," says Ettore. "If we do not find the relic after a thorough search inside, we will turn our attention elsewhere. Perhaps this storm will die down by then."

"Soooo, what? Divide and conquer?" Kylah asks. "What's the best way to do this? Obviously if an Immovable attacks, we want to be together. On the other hand, even a caved-in tunnel won't stop Lin forever."

Ettore glances aside at an empty souvenir shop. Wringing his hands together for warmth, he replies, "Both valid points. I think we should break into groups of two. Then we have some advantage in numbers while also tripling the amount of ground we cover. I will take Sophia—Bixby too, I suppose."

"Kira and me can take Gabe with us," Kylah says.

Micah glances at Dario and grumbles, "Guess that makes us a team."

"Remember," says Ettore, "look for the Greek letters. They might be our only chance to find the Hallowed Vault. We will meet back here in one hour."

The parties split. Sophia and Ettore make for the right side of the open room. She wishes she would have objected to the division of teams. If they're attacked, she and Ettore the least capable of putting up a solid fight—besides Gabriel, of course.

Ettore must notice her reluctance, because he offers his reassurance, saying, "We will be fine. We have Bixby with us. He can smell trouble well before we would!"

Sophia remembers how useful Bixby was when the old man attacked her in Denver. The dog had been brave, sure, but completely ineffective. His presence now doesn't help her feel any better about the situation, but she keeps her mouth shut about it.

Their search takes them away from the central room and down a flight of stairs. Now belowground, they wander by the glow of Ettore's flashlight through the visitor center's various museum exhibits. They eventually find themselves creeping downward through a sloped tunnel called the Cave of Lights. Whether the tunnel was carved by people or by nature, Sophia can't be certain. Its walls and ceilings are bare rock, and miniature exhibits on both sides of the tunnel depict the evolution of human life in Norway.

An eerie stillness lingers within the dark corridor. The fury of the
storm above them doesn't reach this far into the earth. Here, all is
silent. Dead.

Before long, they find an opening in the tunnel's righthand wall.
A placard informs them that they have come to St. John's Chapel.
When they go inside, they discover a tiny alcove built for religious
visitors to the North Cape. There isn't much to it: a dozen wooden
chairs, two candlestands, and an altar, all overlooked by a miniature,
spread-armed figure of Jesus Christ.

Ettore scrutinizes the stone floor and walls for any sign of the
Hallowed Vault's entrance. Sophia, meanwhile, approaches the altar.
It is a beautiful piece, carved from a single, solid block of wood. Narrow at its base, it wings upward and outward with gentle curves, like
the bottom part of an egg that's been cut in half. Its flat, oval surface
holds a used candle and an open Bible.

Sophia lifts the book gently from the altar. She flips absentmindedly through a few pages, admiring the Norwegian script with
its strange letters and vowel markers.

But it is the altar, not the book, which suddenly catches her eye.

"Ettore!" she cries. "Look!"

"What is it?" he replies.

"Here! On the altar, where the Bible was!" she says, tapping the
wooden surface excitedly. "It looks like the letter *E!* Like in *Antikythera!*"

Ettore peers down at Sophia's discovery. Her claim is true. There,
burned into the flat surface, is an elongated character:

But Ettore seems less thrilled by Sophia's breakthrough. She finds his grin rather condescending as he says, "It was a good thought, Sophia. Unfortunately, there is no letter *E* in the word *Antikythera*. Where we put an *E,* the Greeks used an *eta,* remember? And *eta* appears more like a capital *H*. I'm sorry, but we will have to keep looking."

Sophia feels stupid. If she would have taken half a second to remember what Ettore taught them on the boat, she wouldn't have made such an embarrassing mistake.

"It must be a manufacturer's mark," Ettore continues in explanation. "A sort of signature."

Sophia waves her hand dismissively. "No, I get it. Let's keep looking."

Their search takes them back into the tunnel. For the next hour, she and Ettore scour every nook and cranny along the Cave of Lights, but they find nothing. No relic. No Immovable. Not a single clue.

Defeated, Ettore decides it is time to turn back.

As they make their way up the tunnel, Sophia's mind wanders to the dangers they face here. For all they know, an Immovable still lurks in the shadows, waiting to pick them off one by one. Perhaps some of their friends have already been hurt—or worse.

She wonders next about Lin Lai. Certainly the blocked tunnel has slowed down their unseen enemy. But she sailed all the way across the Atlantic for her treasure. She will undoubtedly figure out a way around one obstacle. How soon until she shows up at the North Cape? What will happen if she arrives while Ettore's crew is still here?

Sophia glances up at the man walking beside her. As if struck by a bolt of the cyclone's lightning, she realizes there's an important part of Ettore's story she does not yet know.

"What happened? With you and Lin?" she asks. Her voice is heavy with hesitation. She knows the question is a very personal one.

Ettore looks sideways at her, weighing the question—and its answer—carefully. Finally, he says, "We were in love once."

"You were?" Sophia reacts, shocked to hear such words. "What happened?"

"Lin was the first person I met after the time slip," Ettore recounts. "She was the daughter of a Chinese ambassador to Rome. That's where I found her, in Rome, confused and alone. We teamed up for a while. Together we learned about the Antikythera Device and dedicated ourselves to finding it and learning its secrets. Somewhere along the way, we fell in love. And then, somewhere else along the way, it became apparent that our goals were ... incompatible."

"What do you mean?" Sophia asks.

"I wanted to use the device to return to my family, my work. To set time right again."

A sudden weariness settles over Ettore's features. He looks like someone who has seen a lifetime of sadness and pain as he says, "But she had dark purposes. Evil plans. Love was my motivation. Power was hers."

"Power? How could someone get power from a time machine?" wonders Sophia.

"There are ways," Ettore answers cryptically. "Terrible ways."

"But *how?*" asks the prying girl.

"Sophia," Ettore says with a wistful grin, "I would not burden your innocent and beautiful mind with those answers. I would not do it, even if it meant all the relics were mine by the end of this sentence."

Sophia frowns. Sometimes she forgets that, to the rest of the group, she is still nothing more than a little girl. And little girls can't possibly understand or handle the same things adults do.

I flew a plane, she thinks, her irritation bubbling close to the surface. *I was almost stabbed to death. But go ahead. Pretend I'm some naïve princess who isn't ready to know about the world.*

She stops herself and takes a calming breath. That old bitterness sneaks up on her so easily. She reminds herself that Ettore is simply trying to be kind, trying to protect her in the way that seems right to him. For that, at least, she cannot be angry.

Drawing deep from the wells of her compassion, she says, "I'm sorry you had to go through that. It must have hurt to watch someone you loved turn into that kind of person. And even then, it must have hurt to leave her."

"More than I ever thought possible," Ettore whispers with choked words.

"But now you have lots of people to love," she reminds him. "And lots of people who love you."

"Thank you for saying that, Sophia," Ettore replies as they come to the Cave of Lights' exit. "Sometimes it is easy for me to forget such a simple joy."

They walk the rest of the way in silence, until they have returned to the spacious central room. The other groups are already waiting there.

Everyone looks defeated.

"I take it you found as much as we did," says Ettore.

"Nothing," Micah confirms. "Even if we did, we wouldn't know, because we got no idea what we're lookin' for! If only we coulda got to the map room before Lin. But without the book, we're like pigs tryin' to find acorns in a snowstorm!"

"What now, Ettore?" Kylah asks. She's a kind human being, but Sophia senses a mutinous tone even in the kickboxer's voice.

The Italian says nothing. Turning from the group, he meanders to the north-facing wall of windows. There, he stares out at the bare rock, the torrential rain, and the cliffside globe monument beyond the glass.

"We are all tired and disappointed," the Italian finally says, "but do not let that discourage you. We have made more progress than you might realize."

"And what good has it been?" Dario hisses angrily through his teeth. "We didn't find the book, we don't have the relic, and before long Lin and her people will show up. What then, Ettore?"

"I hope to be long gone by then," he replies. There is more edge in his tone than usual. "But it is growing dark, and we need sleep. The weather, I hope, will be calmer tomorrow. Then we can widen our search to include the outbuildings, as well as the cliffsides and various points of interest."

Nobody seems pleased with the plan, but they're too tired to argue. Murmuring their grumbles, they set up camp in the souvenir shop. From here they can keep an eye on the entrance. And, with only one way in or out of the shop, no one will be able to sneak up behind them. They share a meager meal of dried fruits and nuts, plus some fish jerky Kira discovered in the shop. After eating, Micah leaves to keep watch at the front door, and the rest fall asleep one by one.

Except for Sophia. Long after the snores and rhythmic breathing of the others have filled the room, she lies awake. Listening to the wind howl outside, she is thankful for the shelter.

But it isn't the storm keeping her awake. It's the Greek letters of that word—*Antikythera*—which she can't stop thinking about. Ten letters, but eleven relics. How can each Hallowed Vault be marked by a letter if there aren't enough? Would whoever created them have simply left one blank?

None of it makes sense. Perhaps it means the information in Ettore's books is just plain wrong. Or maybe it was written to send any relic-seekers on a false trail, a wild goose chase.

Or maybe, she realizes, they played an entirely different trick.

Sophia's eyelids pop open with the sudden revelation—at least, she *hopes* it's a revelation.

In Greek, the *th* sound in the word *Antikythera* is made up of a single letter—*theta*. She pictures, floating in the darkness above her, the number zero with a horizontal line slashed through the middle:

Next, she visualizes chopping it in half from top to bottom. What's left? A long, rounded letter *E*.

Just like the one on the altar.

Chapter Sixteen

THE CRUELTIES AND COMFORTS OF LIN LAI

SOPHIA FUMBLES IN THE DARK for her penlight. She clicks it on to make sure it works, then turns it off again just as quickly. Silently, she slides from her sleeping bag, glancing around at the others as she does.

They're sound asleep. Good. In case her theory is wrong, she doesn't want them to see what she's up to.

Bixby raises his head. When he sees his mistress stirring, he grudgingly starts getting up too.

Sophia raises a hand and shakes her head. She motions for him to lie down again, a command he is more than happy to obey.

Micah is still on guard duty. He's stationed in the building's entryway, but his attention is focused on potential lurkers *outside* the walls, not inside. The raging storm easily covers the sound of Sophia's footsteps as she sneaks past him. Frantic with excitement over her possible discovery, she hurries to the tunnel she explored earlier with Ettore. Without considering the dangers of going by herself, she returns to the quiet chapel.

Sophia picks up the Bible and looks at the altar to make sure she wasn't dreaming. Just as she remembered, there is the rounded *E.*

But how is she supposed to get inside the altar? Hack it apart with an axe? Or is there a secret door somewhere in its side? She decides to start with option two. *Much* quieter.

Penlight in hand, she scans the top and front of the altar but finds nothing. She tries moving the candlestands on either side of it, hoping to engage some kind of trapdoor. Still, nothing. She even squeezes between the altar and the wall, praying she will find something on its backside, but the results are the same.

Sophia feels like an idiot. There was never anything here. She was so desperate to be right, especially after the piloting fiasco. She wanted Ettore and the rest to stop seeing her as a dumb little girl. That must be why she invented this crazy idea about the *E* on the altar.

She starts to get up. There's nothing left to do but return to the gift shop and her sleeping bag.

Then she stops. Her hand, planted near the base of the altar, feels something. It's almost like a breeze, a draft between one open space and another.

It isn't inside *the altar,* she realizes with astonishment. *The relic is* under *it!*

Placing her back against the altar and her feet against the wall, Sophia pushes with all her might. At first nothing happens. Then, ever so slowly, the altar slides backward. Inch by inch, with each surging of her strength, she shoves it away from the wall. When she can push no more, she clambers to her feet and looks proudly down into the hole she has uncovered.

It isn't large, a square only about twenty inches long on each side. The "ladder" down is made of handholds and footholds sculpted directly into the stone itself.

She knows she should wake Ettore and the others. This is their victory too. But how much more satisfying will it be when she shows up and drops the relic right onto his lap? Then he'll learn to treat her less like a dumb kid and more like an equal.

With the penlight in her mouth, Sophia descends into the hole. The room below is roughly the same size and shape as the chapel above, but with a slightly lower ceiling. A few dark holes in the walls emit low moans like the mouths of tortured spirits. Other than these, the Hallowed Vault is featureless—except, of course, for the stone pedestal on the opposite end of the room.

Sophia takes a deep breath and approaches it.

There's something on top of the pedestal. Something small and round. And flimsier than she expected.

Her heart sinks. This is no relic. Instead, propped onto its side, is a rolled-up, mildewy piece of paper.

"You've *got* to be kidding me," Sophia whispers aloud.

She picks up the paper gently, as if it might disintegrate at her touch. Placing the penlight back into her mouth so she can use both hands, she gingerly unrolls the brittle slip.

Inside are handwritten words. Whoever wrote it has left a short, cryptic poem:

> *Unmoving I am, yet moved on have I—*
> *The relic with me—where the cliff dwellers fly*
> *Gone back to the house that lights my heart best*
> *The most extreme point 'twixt the north and the west*
> *Find me there, if you dare, and possess the wit*
> *To locate a land where the continents split*
> *Should you be the one who mends time again*
> *I wait where the fire and the ice jointly reign*

Sophia stares at the note in disbelief. After everything they've gone through, the relic isn't here anymore? Even worse! The only clue they have is some dumb riddle! A "land where continents split"? Where "fire and ice jointly reign"? How are they expected to find such a place? And even if they could find this "land," how much more searching will be required to find the relic there?

She reads the poem a second time, and a new detail jumps out at her. The Immovable who wrote this poem spoke of "one who mends time again." What on earth could *that* mean? Sophia is utterly bewildered. Could there really be a person out there who possesses some kind of time-healing superpower?

The scavenger hunt continues, she tells herself with a sigh.

At least she doesn't have to figure out the answers alone. She rolls up the paper so she can bring it to the others, then begins climbing the ladder out of the Hallowed Vault.

But the moment Sophia's face emerges from the hole, her hair is seized and her head yanked back. Before she can cry out in pain and surprise, she feels steel, cold and sharp, against her throat.

A high, chilling voice pierces the darkness. "Out of the hole. Keep your hands where I can see them."

Sophia does what she is told.

Once she is on solid ground, the cruel voice behind her orders, "Give me that paper if you want to live. *Now.*"

She doesn't have to wonder who this is, wrenching back her hair and pressing a knife to her throat. This is no Immovable. An Immovable would stab her and be done with it.

Even before she turns to stare into the dark eyes, Sophia knows Lin Lai has found her.

"That was easier than I expected," Lin says with a sneer, plucking the poem from the girl's outstretched fingers. With one hand she holds the knife against Sophia's neck, while she clumsily unrolls the paper with the other. Silently, she reads it.

"Y-you got what you wanted," Sophia stutters. "Please, just let me go."

"Let you go?" Lin's mocks. "No. I'm afraid I will not be letting you go. You see, you are my leverage."

"I'm your what?"

"My *leverage*," repeats Lin. "As long as I have you, Ettore won't touch me."

Horror floods Sophia's heart when she realizes Lin Lai's intentions.

She is to be taken prisoner.

"This way," Lin snarls, pushing her back into the tunnel.

Sophia wants to scream for help, wants to run. But she knows if she does, it will end with her lying dead in the Cave of Lights.

How could she have been so foolish? She let her ego stand in the way of better judgment with the plane, and now she has done the same thing at the North Cape. Why didn't she wake them up? Why didn't she bring anyone with her?

Because she had something to prove. But the only thing she's proven is how useless she really is.

Back in the main chamber of the visitor center, they approach the entryway doors. There Sophia sees the faint outline of Micah. He's sprawled on the ground, either dead or unconscious. In little more than a week, he has become like a big brother to her, and her heart weeps as she guesses his fate.

She expects that Lin will force her immediately through the doors and away from the North Cape Hall. Instead, Lin shoves her past the entryway toward the souvenir shop.

Here Lin stops, clears her throat, and in a singsong tone calls out,

"Wake up, wake up, Ettore! I have something I must show you!"

Sophia hears the rustling of sleeping bags in the darkness. Moments later, Ettore stands in front of them, lit faintly by the glow of Sophia's penlight. Behind him stand the shadowy forms of the twins and Dario.

Suddenly, Bixby springs forward out of the gloom, snarling and snapping, to his mistress's defense. Before Sophia realizes what's happening, her faithful dog lunges at Lin's midsection.

There is a heavy blow, followed by a canine shriek. The well-timed stroke of Lin's iron fist sends Bixby careening to the floor. He twitches once in a final attempt to rescue his best friend, then lies deathly still.

In an instant, everything breaks inside Sophia. Her body convulses with sobs, and tears are soon wetting her captor's knife-wielding hand.

Lin ignores Sophia's blubbering. All her attention is fixed upon Ettore. Getting right down to business, she says, "You should learn to keep your pawns closer, *my love*. I know they are expendable pieces, but lose too many and you leave yourself exposed. Vulnerable."

"Let her go, Lin," Ettore pleads. "This doesn't concern her."

"Whether it does or doesn't, here is what happens now," says Lin. "I am leaving with the clue"—She flourishes the Immovable's poem like it's a banner of victory—"*and* with this girl."

Aside to Sophia, Lin whispers, "What is your name?"

"Sophia," she replies miserably.

"I am leaving with my new friend Sophia," Lin announces.

Ettore steps forward, begging, "Lin, please, this is not—"

But Lin continues as if Ettore were mute, and his words no louder than a mime's. She declares, "You will not follow us. You will not look for us. If I see you, your boat, or any of your people again, this girl will pay for your mistake with her life. Stay away, and she stays alive. Do you understand?"

For a moment, Ettore does nothing. He simply stares at her. Even in the darkness, there is no mistaking the blend of grief, pity, and disgust in his gaze.

Then, slowly, he nods his agreement.

"For once, a wise move," Lin says. To Sophia she mutters, "Say your goodbyes, girl."

But instead of saying her goodbyes, Sophia does something else. At the top of her lungs, she shouts, "Go to the land where continents split!"

"Shut up!" Lin snarls, pressing the knife against Sophia's throat and yanking her backward.

But Sophia won't be stopped. She has realized that she too possesses a tiny bit of leverage.

Lin can't kill her now. Maybe later, but not yet. If she does, Ettore and the rest will swarm and overpower her in moments.

"It's where fire and ice reign!" the girl screams, even as her throat's movements cause the blade to dig into her skin. She tries to remember something else—*anything* else—and again cries out, "Go where the cliff dwellers fly!"

"I. Said. Shut. *Up!*" Lin seethes. Hauling Sophia past Bixby's and Micah's bodies, she hurries them through the North Cape Hall's front doors.

The world explodes around them. The storm's rampage is worse than ever. Tiny pellets of rain, now frozen into sleet, sting Sophia's bare face and arms. Fully immersed in the cyclone's fury, Lin drags her past the parking lot and a short distance down the road. Here, hidden behind one of the outbuildings, waits a car. Lin throws open the driver's door, then hurls the girl roughly across the center console and into the passenger seat. She herself slides hurriedly inside and locks the car.

In a desperate attempt to escape, Sophia presses her door's *unlock* button. She will make a run for it, even if she dies trying.

Nothing happens.

"Safety locks," Lin explains with a dark grin. "Do not try to escape again. That was your second strike."

"Second? What was the first?" Sophia asks indignantly.

"Shouting the clues to Ettore," Lin answers. "You don't want to learn what happens when you strike out. Now, keep your hands folded behind your head. I will not tolerate any further trouble from you."

Lin drives them back along the winding North Cape road to its end. There, instead of turning south toward the rest of Norway, she heads north.

"Where are we going?" Sophia whimpers. Oddly, she feels tired more than anything.

"My ship," Lin replies without taking her eyes off the road. "It is docked beside a little village. My crew is waiting and ready to leave the moment we are onboard."

"And then where? Do you know what the clue means? Do you know where to go?"

"I do. And thanks to you, Ettore will also know." Lin's tone is steely and menacing. "For your sake, I pray he does not come after us."

The road begins dropping back toward the sea, and before long they come into a village. The name on the welcome sign is one Sophia has seen before.

Skarsvåg. This is where Dario planned to take them before the weather turned wild. Yet Lin Lai was crazy enough to sail through the worst of the cyclone to get here.

What else would she be crazy enough to do?

As Lin parks the car next to the dock, Sophia makes out the rough details of a yacht floating alongside it. It's much larger than the one she took from New York to Norway. Some actor or politician or famous billionaire must have owned it once upon a time, because through its lighted windows she sees nothing but extravagance. Only the richest people dropped that much money on things no one would ever need.

"Out," Lin barks.

Sophia obeys.

Outside, Lin leads her to the gangplank which bridges the gap between dock and boat. She forces Sophia up the ramp first, thus putting a stop to any last-ditch escape attempt. At the top of the gangplank, Lin reaches over Sophia's shoulder and pounds on the door.

It opens, and light floods over them. Lin shoves her inside, and the door closes behind them.

Sophia wipes the water from her eyes, then looks up at the man who opened the door.

His eyes are wide with surprise. Certainly he didn't expect to see a second dripping-wet person come through the door.

"Thank you, Redbeard," Lin says. Her tone more cordial than before. "Go tell Cook and Columbia that we must leave immediately."

Redbeard—Sophia has a hunch that isn't the name on his birth certificate—is towering and musclebound. It's easy to see how he earned his nickname, for both hair and beard are rust red, as well as curly and untended. He has rich, loamy eyes which stare at Lin almost reverently, as if he were receiving orders from the Pope or a president.

"Where shall I tell them we're goin'," he asks in a deep and thickly accented voice.

Lin casts a sideways glance at Sophia, then says, "I suppose it can't hurt to let you know now." Her gaze returns to Redbeard. "Tell them to make for Iceland."

Sophia feels like kicking herself. How many times has she read about Iceland and dreamed of going there? It's a land of glaciers and volcanoes, of snowfields and geysers. A place where both fire and ice do indeed reign together. Her panicked mind was too unfocused to work out the clues back at the North Cape.

It doesn't matter now. Even if Ettore and the others deduce Lin's destination based on the snippets Sophia yelled at them, there's no guarantee they will come for her. What if Lin's threat was enough to dissuade them? What if they never find her, and she remains in the clutches of a lunatic woman until she is either dead or abandoned in some remote land?

"Come with me," Lin snaps, jolting Sophia from her waking nightmare.

For the first time since their initial encounter in the chapel, they find themselves in decent lighting, and Sophia takes a long look at her captor as they march down the marble-tiled hallway. Lin Lai has straight, jet-black hair, most of which is pulled back in a tight bun. Only a few strands hang loose over her dark eyes and petite nose. Her skin is fair and has a princess-like flawlessness. If Sophia had first seen her in a different context, she might have thought Lin looked sweet and harmless. But with an array of knives strapped to her belt and metal-plated gloves on her hands—Sophia understands now why Bixby was knocked senseless so easily—Lin Lai is a warrior goddess.

Lin halts in front of a door. She produces a set of keys from her jacket pocket and fits one into the lock.

Sophia expects to find the darkest, dingiest closet on the other side. Instead, Lin ushers her into a bedroom as luxurious as the rest of the yacht. There is a king bed, a television, and a dresser. In one corner is a bathroom, complete with the largest shower Sophia has ever seen. On the far side of the room, French doors exit onto a private balcony.

"You will stay here during our voyage," Lin informs her. "I think you will be comfortable, if not spoiled. Feel free to breathe fresh air on the balcony if you like. You may use the television, bathroom, and whatever else you find in here."

"Thanks," Sophia mumbles.

"I altered the door," Lin continues, "so that it locks and unlocks from the outside. There will also be a guard out there, so don't even think of trying to escape. If you do, and I catch you—which I will—you will trade this stateroom for the ship's septic tank. Do you understand?"

Sophia nods.

"Good. I will speak with you more tomorrow. For now, I must update my crew."

Without another word, Lin spins on her heels and marches from the room. A lock *clicks* into place after the door shuts, and silence envelopes Sophia.

She rushes immediately to the bed, unable to believe what she got away with. Once again, the adults have looked at her and seen only a little girl. Once again, they have underestimated her.

This time, it was all to her advantage.

Reaching down to her hip, Sophia yanks the pistol from its holster. She didn't have the opportunity to use it before—not with a razor-sharp knife at her throat. Nor would it be wise to use it now as they cross the frigid waters of the North Atlantic.

But the time will come. She knows it.

And when it does, she won't hesitate to do what she must.

Sophia stuffs the pistol beneath the mattress. Feeling oddly confident for a girl in a prison, and with nothing better to do, she decides to warm up under a steaming-hot shower.

There, under the camouflage of water, she pours out her quiet tears for Micah and Bixby.

Chapter Seventeen

EMPRESS OF TIME

THE NEXT TIME SOPHIA sees another person, there is already a small stack of watched DVDs scattered on the floor below the television. Her comfortable prison no longer lurches violently back and forth with the waves. The yacht escaped the cyclone hours earlier, and the sky outside is now a rich shade of blue.

A forceful knock awakens Sophia from her catnap. Wearing a fresh shirt she found in the dresser, she rolls out of bed to answer the door. When she turns the handle, it doesn't budge.

She remembers then that the door is locked from the outside, so she calls, "You can come in."

A key fumbles in the lock, and the door opens. The man called Redbeard stands on the other side, looking at her awkwardly.

"Hi—um—Mr. Redbeard," Sophia says shyly.

To her surprise, a tiny grin twitches at the corners of Redbeard's lips. In his thick accent, he replies, "That's just what the others call me—in our group, I mean. We all have nicknames. Seein' as you're not part of our group, you can call me Ewan. That's my real name."

"Okay. What did you want, Mr. Ewan?"

"The Empress wants to see you."

Confused, Sophia raises an eyebrow.

"Uh—Miss Lai, I mean," he stammers.

Sophia finds it amusing that this burly, bearded man is so easily flustered. At the same time, she also wonders why he would refer to Lin as "the Empress."

"What does she want?" Sophia inquires.

He shrugs. "Don't know. She didn't tell me. Just said she wants to talk to you."

Ewan Redbeard's nylon pants *swish* rhythmically as he leads her along the hallway and up a flight of stairs. Just like Lin, he has knives aplenty strapped to his waist, but Sophia wonders if he's truly hardened enough to use them. After they pass through another corridor, they exit into the fresh air and abundant sunlight of the main deck.

Straight ahead is Lin. She leans upon the bow rail, staring forward at the western horizon. Even when Sophia approaches and stands beside her, Lin doesn't break her gaze away from the sea.

"Thank you for joining me," says Lin. Her voice is neither kind nor cruel. She sounds neutral, almost robotic, to the girl standing at her side.

"Didn't have much of a choice," Sophia responds, trying to sound more courageous than she feels.

"Are you scared?" Lin asks.

Sophia shrugs and says, "A little."

"You have no reason for it, so long as you stay in line. Despite what happened at the North Cape, I don't want you afraid of me."

Sophia remains silent. The Lin speaking to her now seems quite different than the one who previously held a knife to her throat.

"Do you know anything about Iceland?" Lin asks, changing the subject.

"Not much," says Sophia, leaning against the railing. "I've seen enough pictures to know it's beautiful. But that's about it."

"Yes. It is beautiful. And harsh, and breathtaking, and destructive," says Lin, glancing down at her for the first time. "Iceland is all of those things. Or rumor says so, at least. I myself have never been there."

"Sounds like what I've heard too," murmurs Sophia.

"Iceland," Lin says, "is rather like a person. Wouldn't you agree?"

Sophia stares up at her. She already feels lost in their conversation. "I don't know what you mean," she says.

"I mean that people are complicated, nuanced," Lin explains. "Just like Iceland. It is full of fire, and it is full of ice. It builds and sculpts and, at the same time, destroys. The same thing is true of people. Nobody can be described accurately using only one word, or ten, or even a hundred. Nobody is *only* evil, or *only* good. *Only* selfless, or *only* wise. We are complicated, complex creatures. There is always more to a person than what first meets the eye. Unless, of course, we shut those eyes."

Lin turns her undivided attention to Sophia and continues. "Yet so often, once we have decided in our own minds who somebody is, we are unwilling to see anything else. Throughout history, human beings have always blinded themselves this way. We see in a person what we want to see, or what others have told us. But the full truth? Including the things we don't want to see? This we are blind toward! We shut our eyes. We close our ears. Because deep down, we know it is easier to remain ignorant. Then we never have to admit that we were wrong about someone. And we never have to confront the fact that we ourselves are complex people. If you can believe that one person is simply evil and nothing more, you can also believe that you yourself are simply good."

"And I'm guessing you want me to think you're ... complicated? Nuanced?" says Sophia. Her tone makes it clear she isn't buying whatever Lin is trying to sell. To drive her point home, she adds, "Instead of just evil and greedy?"

Lin laughs and shakes her head. "I am sure that's what Ettore wants you to think. And, I admit, you wouldn't be entirely wrong to do so. I don't know if I would use the terms *evil* and *greedy* to describe myself, but it is true that I am seeking power and strength in this quest. With a fully functional Antikythera Device, that is exactly what I will have."

She pauses for effect, then says, "Actually, I was speaking more about Ettore. Being nuanced. Complicated. Not exactly what you see on the surface."

"I know enough to know he's not like you," Sophia says in Ettore's defense.

To her surprise, Lin laughs again and replies, "No, he certainly is not! I hide nothing. My goals, my purpose, my *being*—it is all quite straightforward. You say I desire power, and I do not deny it. The Lin Lai you see is Lin Lai as she really is. But Ettore? He may be a gentle and kindhearted man. These were qualities which first attracted me to him. Yet he is also more than that. And less."

"What do you mean?" asks Sophia.

She hates herself for giving in to her curiosity. For swallowing Lin's bait.

"What I mean is this," says Lin, savoring each moment as a tigress would a juicy steak. "Ettore is dishonest."

"Dishonest? Like ... he's a liar?"

"Not a liar. Not exactly," Lin says. "He is more like a person who conveniently covers up the darker parts of himself. The less attractive parts of his past."

Sophia says nothing as she stares out over the water, wondering what Lin could possibly mean.

"What did Ettore tell you?" Lin asks. "About our relationship? About our time together?"

Sophia shrugs. "He told me he met you in Rome. That you started looking for the Antikythera Device together, before you turned all power hungry and he decided to leave you. That's about it."

"Well, Sophia," Lin replies, clearly relishing what she is about to divulge, "let me tell you *my* version of events. Just like Ettore's, it starts in Rome. My parents were foreign ambassadors there. They were emissaries of my country, China, and were intent on forging an alliance of power between our two nations. Though distant from one another, we believed we could possess great strength together. At the time, I attended university in Rome. Like my parents, I was obtaining a degree in foreign relations. I idolized them and wanted to follow in their footsteps."

Sophia can sympathize with the thought. How many times had she wanted to be a dentist like her own mother? Or a police officer like her father? At some point in every child's life, they dream of growing up to be just like mom and dad.

Lin's story continues. "Then, in 1923, shortly after Mussolini's rise to power in Italy, I jumped forward in time. I was on my way home from an educational visit to the Colosseum when everything changed. Suddenly there were no more people, no more cars zipping about. Nothing but empty street after empty street. I was terrified and ran to the embassy, certain I would find my parents. But the embassy was no longer there. A different building existed in its place, and there was no sign of my father or mother. I was alone. Abandoned. Devastated."

"No offense," interrupts Sophia, "but what does this have to do with anything?"

"Be patient. Like all stories, this one has its purpose."

Lin tilts her face toward the azure sky with its puffy clouds. She squints, peering back into her memories.

"Ettore found me three days later," Lin says. "It was a completely chance encounter. I was scouring the city for any sign of life, and my search brought me to the Vatican. I first saw him there, wandering lost and aimless, suitcase clutched tightly in his hand."

Sophia wonders if Lin is referring to the same suitcase Ettore still carries, the one he watches over so carefully. Once again, she finds herself dying to know what's in it.

"He told me he was planning to break into the Vatican's ancient library," Lin says. "For hundreds of years, there have been rumors about the mysteries held inside that library. Ettore informed me there might be one which would allow us to control time itself. If we could discover the secrets, he thought we might return to our homes, our families, and the lives we left behind."

At that moment Lin's story is interrupted by one of her crewmembers. A slender, eggshell-pale woman approaches them and says, "Sorry to interrupt, but I wanted to let you know we were blown further south by the storm than I thought. That will work out, though. We'll be able to anchor safely offshore, and you can take the Zodiac to the mainland. The south is nothing but beaches, so finding a good landing should be easy. We'll be there in three or four days."

Sophia has never heard of a Zodiac before, but she figures it must be some kind of smaller boat held onboard the yacht.

"Is that all, Columbia?" Lin speaks curtly, annoyed at the intrusion into her conversation with Sophia.

"One more thing. There have been absolutely no signs we're being followed," the auburn-haired Columbia says. "If Ettore is coming, he's a long way behind."

Sophia's stomach drops. She feels sick, and it has nothing to do with the sea.

"Thank you," says Lin, grinning wickedly. "Now leave us. I must finish my talk with the girl."

Columbia nods briskly and returns midship.

Without missing a beat, Lin jumps back into her story. "I should have been suspicious from the beginning. Ettore had obviously been there before. He knew exactly where to find the materials we needed. But I became so caught up in our task that I didn't question him. We found book after book devoted to the subject of an ancient time machine called the Antikythera Device. Some of it he dismissed as legend. Other portions he accepted as ironclad truth. But by the time we were done—many months later—two things had happened. Ettore and I had fallen in love, and we had vowed to use our knowledge to find the eleven lost relics."

"He told me about that," Sophia informs her kidnapper. "He wanted to use the machine for good, and you wanted to use it for evil."

"Not quite," Lin retorts sharply. "Not in the beginning, anyway. In the beginning, I wanted to return home. Like you do, I imagine. But then one day, my mind began to itch. I desired to learn what had happened to my parents after my disappearance. So, to my misfortune, I began digging through newspapers and other city records, hoping I might discover their fate. Do you know what I learned?"

Sophia shakes her head.

"They died," Lin says bitterly. "Before the beginning of the Second World War, Benito Mussolini accused them of spying. Of treachery. He had them both shot in the public square."

Unsure how to respond, Sophia's mouth hangs agape.

"That's when I realized that traveling back to my own time would do no good," Lin tells her. "If my parents were killed a few years after my disappearance, why would I use such power—the power of time travel—to return there, only to watch them die?"

"But couldn't you still go back and warn them?" objects Sophia. "Couldn't you help them escape before they were killed?"

"I knew my parents well enough to know they would never believe me," Lin says. "They would only have accused me of inventing fairytales or losing my mind."

"Then what about stopping Mussolini?" suggests Sophia. "Couldn't you do that?"

"The Antikythera Device transports a person through time," replies Lin. "It does not make them invincible, nor does it give them access to well-guarded world leaders."

Sophia grunts her frustration and shouts, "Well, there must be *something* you could do to save them! Besides, anything would be better than what you're doing now."

Lin appraises Sophia's suggestion before she says, "Believe me, I have considered it from all angles. Every version was too risky and filled with potentially disastrous outcomes. In the end, I did the only thing I could: I mourned them. Then, when my tears ran dry, I decided to honor their memory the best way I knew how."

"What do you mean?" Sophia instantly regrets asking the question. She's afraid to hear the answer.

"My parents were dedicated to power," answers Lin. "It was, in a sense, their god. My father's ultimate goal was to become president of the Republic of China. After he seized and consolidated power, my mother would rule alongside him with all the might and grandeur of the ancient emperors and empresses. I would be their heir to rule after them, and my children after me."

"In the end," Lin notes with a wry chuckle, "their dreams were too small for me. The power of the Antikythera Device, I realized, was also the key to seizing power of my own. With the ability to travel through time, I could study the technologies and weaponry of future peoples. Then, wielding their knowledge, I would subjugate the peoples of the past. Not merely those in one period, or two. But in every era of Earth's history."

Though it is a warm afternoon, goosebumps crawl up Sophia's arms.

Lin finally arrives at the climax of her long speech, declaring, "I will become much more than an empress of China. I will become the Empress of Time."

She pauses, savoring the self-appointed name lingering on her lips.

"And," Lin continues, "I told Ettore he would be my emperor. He agreed. Together, hand in hand, we would rule not just the world. We would rule all of *history*."

Hearing this, Sophia shakes her head violently and says, "I don't believe it. I *can't* believe it. Ettore doesn't want that. I know he doesn't!"

"You think you know Ettore," Lin replies darkly, "but there is so much you know nothing about. I have known him deeper than you ever will."

Relishing Sophia's expression of disbelief and denial, Lin says, "Don't worry. I won't spoil all the surprises. I won't tell you what he carries in that suitcase. I won't tell you why he knew so much about the secret library of the Vatican. I won't tell you how he gained such renown as a physicist. No, I want to watch sweet, honorable Ettore sweat and tremble as he reveals those secrets himself. But mark my words, Sophia. Ettore isn't what he seems to be. Behind that gentle, noble exterior lurks something darker. And *that* is his dishonesty. He would have you believe his heart is purer than a child's. But there is a truth he doesn't want you to know. Because if you did—if the rest of his crew knew—you would not waste one more footstep following him."

Sophia's mind feels heavy. She can't listen to another word from Lin's mouth. Abruptly she asks, "Can I go back to my room now?"

Lin doesn't reply immediately. Instead, she gestures toward someone waiting inside.

Redbeard appears, but he doesn't approach them.

"Hide from it all you want," Lin tells her. "But the truth always has its day in the sun."

"Yeah, sure," mumbles Sophia.

Lin grabs her firmly by both shoulders. Leaning in close, she whispers, "If you ever see him again, ask him what is in his suitcase. Ask him how he acquired it. That's all it will take for your image of Ettore Majorana to crumble to pieces."

Sophia yanks herself free from Lin's claws. She won't listen to anything more. Turning away, she marches toward Redbeard.

Before she can think twice about it, she whips around so that she is again facing Lin. A flinty defiance has been building inside her like a pressure cooker, and in that moment, it comes bursting forth.

"You know what?" she cries. "Even if you're telling me the truth, even if Ettore does have this dark past like you say, there's still one huge difference between the two of you."

"Yes? And what is that?" Lin asks, taken aback by Sophia's sudden boldness.

"Remorse. He knew it was wrong, the way he was thinking. And even if some of those ideas are still hiding in his heart, he isn't acting on them. *That's* the difference between you and him. That's what makes him a hundred times the person you are."

Lin glares at her so intensely, Sophia wonders if she'll be tossed overboard. Then Lin breaks into a grin of dark amusement, like that of a kid frying ants with a magnifying glass.

"You know, Sophia," she says, taking slow and deliberate strides toward her captive, "I admire you. You have more courage than any girl I have ever met. I could use someone like you among my attendants. With a little work, you could become my second-in-command. The *Princess* of Time."

Sophia stares at her with revulsion. For a moment, she is lost for words. Then she says, "I wouldn't join you in a million years. Not even if you made me princess of the entire universe."

With that final statement, she turns and marches to the door.

Redbeard is waiting there, wearing a curious expression. He can't believe someone would speak to Lin that way and live to tell the tale.

"We're done," Sophia tells him. "You can take me back to my room."

Chapter Eighteen

THE LAND OF FIRE AND ICE

ISOLATION IS THE APPARENT punishment for Sophia's defiance, for she spends the remainder of the voyage in her room. Lin doesn't summon her for any additional above-decks conversations. The only times Sophia sees another human face are when meals are delivered by a stocky, rosy-cheeked woman named Caesar.

With little else to do, she whittles away her time exercising and practicing the kickboxing skills she learned from Kira and Kylah. She also frequents her balcony, doing nothing but staring out at the sea and thinking. Her mind wanders again and again to Bixby and Micah. She doesn't know whether they are dead or alive or struggling somewhere in between. She wonders whether her friends will come for her, and if they do, whether Lin will fulfill her threat by executing Sophia.

Mostly she dreams of home. She's surprised at herself when she realizes she misses her motorhome, her bed—even her stupid chickens. She's living out the adventure she always wanted, but now that she is, her heart longs for the comfort and constancy of her old life.

Just as Columbia predicted, the coastline of Iceland is within reach three days later. Instead of docking straightaway, they sail westward along the southern coast. From her balcony, Sophia gapes at the immense arms of white glaciers. They are frozen rivers, flowing down the high mountains in slow motion, hugging the lower slopes of green and brown and gray. Below these the coastline seems to be one long, continuous beach. Its sand isn't white like in America. Here it is dark as coal. Sophia knows these black sand beaches exist because of all the volcanoes in Iceland, which have been belching up burnt stuff from the belly of the earth for countless ages.

A few hours after arriving at the coast, the yacht slows to a stop. The rhythmic clanking of metal echoes throughout the vessel. Sophia assumes this means they are dropping the anchors.

She retrieves the pistol and holster from beneath her pillow, returning them to their hiding place at her hip. The gray sky and low clouds outside have convinced her to dress warm, so she puts on a fur-lined coat. Beneath her pants, she adds a layer of leggings.

Redbeard fetches her a few minutes later and leads her to an on-board movie theater. Lin is standing by the large screen, looking down at the rest of her crew occupying the seats. Columbia and Caesar are the only ones Sophia recognizes. There are an additional three men and one woman she has never seen.

Lin beckons for Sophia to approach her. She also wears a fur-lined coat and is dressed for cold weather. A black bow leans against the wall behind her, and on the floor by her feet is a forest green backpack.

Sophia doesn't have to look inside to know what it must hold.

The fabled Book of Relics.

"Allow me to introduce everyone," Lin says, clutching the girl's shoulder with a talon-like grip. "This is Sophia, the girl I liberated from Ettore's company."

Nobody waves or even mouths a simple "hello" to her.

Lin points to a wiry, rodent-looking man with beady eyes and a scraggly beard. His face matches his nickname. Lin introduces him as Mouse.

The tall, gaunt fellow next to him she calls Stoker. He cringes when he hears the nickname. It's obvious to Sophia that the vampire-faced man is not a fan.

Next down the line is a young woman with light freckles and vibrant bronze skin. She is called Cook. Sophia remembers hearing the name when she first came aboard the yacht in Skarsvåg.

Finally, there is a pudgy man of Asian descent who speaks with an elegant British accent. He is known simply as Q.

As soon as introductions are over, Lin orders Sophia to sit, then cuts to the chase.

A map of Iceland illuminates the movie screen. Sophia thinks the island looks almost like a bird or a dragon. Its main bulk serves as the body, while a protrusion in the northwest forms its head and neck.

Pointing at a spot smackdab in the middle of the southern coast, Lin says, "Currently, we are somewhere near here."

She shifts her hand to indicate the many-fingered peninsula jutting out from Iceland's northwest corner—the dragon's head. "But we need to go *here*."

Suddenly, two lines from the Immovable's poem strike Sophia: *Gone back to the house that lights my heart best ... The most extreme point 'twixt the north and the west.*

"This," Lin informs them, "is the district of Iceland called the West Fjords. Since you all are familiar with the poem, you must realize it makes sense that the Immovable took the relic here."

She pauses, waiting for questions. Hearing none, she proceeds to share the plan. "Cook and Columbia will wait offshore with the boat. The rest of us, including Sophia, will ride ashore on the Zodiac. Once there, we will find a pair of vehicles. Then, when we have secured our transportation, we will begin traveling westward."

At this point, Caesar raises a hand and asks, "How will we know where to look when we get there? There must be a billion places the relic could be hiding!"

"We will use our brains and our patience," Lin replies. "None of us knows much about this island. For that reason, I'm afraid we will have to stop at a school or a library, or perhaps even a tourist shop to do some research. With any luck, we will discover the exact location identified by the Immovable's poem. And once we do, the relic will be ours. Any other questions?"

If the crew has any, they don't ask them.

Lin nods her head briskly and says, "Good. Now, off to the Zodiac. I must have a word with Sophia."

When the rest have gone, Lin sits beside the girl and says, "Against the wishes of several of my attendants, I am going to make a deal with you."

"Okay?" replies Sophia, wondering where Lin is going with this "deal."

"I will allow you a certain amount of freedom as we travel," Lin explains. "I will not tie your hands or your feet. I will not blindfold you. I will not post a guard to watch your every move. When we stop, you are free to roam about the area as you choose. I don't care."

"And what do you want from me?" asks Sophia.

"In return," says Lin, "you will behave. You will not try to escape. You will not harm me or my people in any way. If you are asked to help with something, you will help. Do you agree?"

It feels dirty to make any kind of agreement with someone like Lin Lai. But Sophia can see no disadvantage for herself, so she nods her acceptance.

"Good," says Lin. "Do I need to tell you what will happen if you break the agreement?"

Sophia shakes her head. "No, I remember. Septic tank."

Ten minutes later, Sophia is skipping across the waves on the Zodiac. The inflatable motorboat didn't seem very seaworthy to her at first, but it is sturdier and faster than it looks. Within minutes, Redbeard and Mouse are pulling the rest of them up onto the dry sand.

Sophia clambers out and blinks. The whipping wind has already dried out her eyes, which she imagines must look something like tiny white-and-green raisins. Ahead, through her crusty corneas, she spots a road. There is also a bridge spanning a dark, swift river filled with odd bluish boulders. As she and Lin's crew come nearer, she realizes the strange "rocks" are actually boulder-sized chunks of ice floating down the stream to the sea.

The party of seven climbs up the embankment to the road. Here, Sophia's mouth drops. Spread before her is a vision which must have been transported to Earth from some fantasy world. A vast, silvery-blue lake has made its home here, only a couple hundred yards from the sea. Floating steadily upon the lake is a city of ice.

They are the broken hunks of glaciers. Some of these sapphire-streaked icebergs are jagged and angular, while others are graceful with elegant curves. Many are so massive, they make her Colorado mansion look like a dollhouse. Dozens of smaller ice chunks have congregated near the mouth of the outflowing stream. When the sun has melted them enough, they will enter the final leg of their journey as the stream carries them to the sea. There they will become one again with the oceans, from which they first came so long ago.

The great ships of ice hypnotize Sophia. She can't look away. Can't miss this beauty for a single second. As Lin leads them to a large parking lot on the other side of the road, Sophia stumbles behind the group, hardly noticing where her feet are taking her. Even when she is seated in the back of a steel-blue Saab driven by Redbeard, she gazes longingly upon the lake, like one who has received a glimpse of heaven itself.

Then they round a curve. The lake disappears, and its spell is broken. Only its memory will remain with her until her dying day.

Which, she hopes, won't be *too* soon.

Back and forth, the highway winds lazily along the coast. As they weave westward, the landscape outside Sophia's window changes dramatically. One moment they find themselves driving through lush, grassy tundra; a mile later, through blackened earth with twisted groves of volcanic rock. Near Iceland's southernmost point, they pass a prominent cliff jutting out into the sea. At its furthest tip is a great stone archway, a door which giants of old might have passed through during a trip along the coast.

Eventually, the road turns north. The late afternoon sun peeks at them from behind the clouds, promising a warmer tomorrow. Their journey now takes them across a stretch of flat, green country dotted by farmhouses. In one field, Sophia watches a herd of stout, shaggy Icelandic horses galloping merrily across their territory. Elsewhere there are flocks of sheep, thriving even without human intervention and care.

Everyone is so captivated by the landscape, they forget to keep their guard up.

The attack comes from nowhere. One moment they're enjoying the unrivaled beauty of creation. The next, they're spinning out of control. The shriek of crumpling, twisting metal rings through their ears, drowning out their own screams. Redbeard seizes the steering wheel, straining to regain control. He's unsuccessful. The car careens off the road, rolls once, and comes to a stop.

All three jump out, dazed but uninjured.

Lin's backpack is already in her arms. This confirms Sophia's earlier suspicion that it must contain something extremely valuable. Only the Book of Relics could be so important.

Looking back, Sophia sees that the car carrying the other four has suffered a similar fate. It, too, blew out its tires and ran off the road, where it crashed headfirst into a large boulder.

Before anyone in the other car can even open a door, a swarm of burly, fur-clad men surrounds them. It's hard to tell how many, but Sophia guesses there are at least a dozen.

It turns out Iceland isn't so unpopulated after all.

The car doors are all but ripped off their hinges. Polished axes, knives, and swords flash in the afternoon sunlight. Among the hands of the bearded assailants, thick ropes flail wildly.

In seconds, Stoker is yanked from the vehicle, bound and gagged. His attackers haul him to his feet and throw him against the truck. Caesar is quick to follow. Blood gushes from a gash above her temple, and her eyes are wide with terror.

But Sophia can only guess at the fates of Mouse and Q. Eight of the wild men have now turned their attention to the other car. Brandishing their weapons, they charge forward, either to kill or to capture.

Lin lunges for the trunk, cursing herself for stowing her bow inside it while they drove. But the trunk door was crushed and twisted when the Saab rolled off the roadway. She tries only once to open it, but the mangled metal doesn't budge.

In frustration, Lin slams her fist against the trunk door. Then she hisses a single command: "Run!"

Redbeard glances at her in disbelief. "We can't just leave them!" he shouts.

"We cannot fight our way through so many," Lin argues. "To try would be suicide. I order you again—*run!*"

Murderous war cries pursue them as they race across the spongy, uneven tundra. An arrow whistles past Sophia's head, followed shortly by a second. When a knife thrown by one of the wild men glances off Lin's shoulder, Sophia knows their assailants must be closing the gap.

As she runs, the pistol bounces against her hip. She certainly wasn't planning to reveal her secret here and now. She wanted to wait until she could be sure it would help her escape Lin Lai. She also doubts whether her partial magazine—twelve measly bullets—would be enough to stop the horde of ferocious men.

"There's a farmhouse ahead!" Redbeard shouts. "See it on the slope? If you can reach it, you might be able to make a stand."

"*You?*" Lin screams back at him. "What do you mean, '*you*'?"

"I'll split away and draw some of them off," yells Redbeard. Another arrow passes close enough to nick his ear with its fletching. "Good luck!"

Before Lin can protest further, he's gone. Glancing aside, Sophia sees him angling back toward the road. At least three of the men have taken the bait and are pursuing him instead.

An agonized cry erupts on Sophia's left side.

Lin stumbles to the ground, a feathered shaft embedded below her right shoulder blade.

Sophia hesitates. This is her chance. She can keep running. Let the wild men finish Lin off. Sure, some might follow Sophia, but probably few enough that she can take them down with the pistol.

And then ... freedom.

Before she realizes what she's doing, Sophia throws herself onto the ground beside Lin. She reaches to her hip.

Five wooly attackers are bearing down on them. There is no time to stop and think.

There is only time to act.

CRACK! CRACK! CRACK! A half-dozen shots split the air like thunder.

Two men drop dead to the tundra. Another buckles to his knees but remains upright. Four and five charge onward, angling toward her from both sides to pin her between them. One raises an axe above his head, the other a thick broadsword.

Sophia fires another short volley, and the axe-man falls.

But the last one is too close, and she's facing the wrong direction. His sword arm is already dropping toward her. She doesn't have enough time to swing the gun around.

There is only one thing she can do.

She kicks him—*hard*—just like Kira and Kylah taught her. Her heel catches him in his great barrel of a belly. The force of his charge throws her off-balance and onto the ground, but her blow also stuns him momentarily.

That's all the time she needs. Sucking in a deep breath, she aims the pistol, and fires twice.

The man drops backward, dead.

Sophia exhales with relief, but a moment too soon.

A shadow falls over her. She hears a bone-chilling cry of wrath. Turns. Sees the hulking form of the axe man.

She thought she had killed him.

Now his axe is slicing downward. Falling toward her kneeling form. In that moment, Sophia knows her earthly journey has come to its end.

As when the old man almost killed her back in Denver, she wonders what dying will feel like.

She squeezes her eyes shut.

But the deathblow never comes.

When she dares to open her eyes again, the man is stumbling backward. Two knives, both with identical handles, protrude from his chest.

Lin is standing beside her. The feathered arrow in her back rises and falls with her belabored breathing, and she stares down at the man she just stabbed.

He sinks to his knees, snarling defiantly. Then his eyes roll up into his head, and he collapses facedown upon the earth.

A moment later, Lin does the same. The arrow protrudes above her like a tiny flagpole planted in her back.

Sophia scrambles to Lin's side and leans in close. She's alive, but her breaths are shallow. Rattling.

Again, the debate rages within her. She knows what she *should* do. She should leave Lin for dead. Sophia can go on alone, hunt down the relic herself.

But the annoying ethical voice inside her won't shut up. She knows she can't leave anyone, not even an enemy, wounded and dying like this.

"Get up!" Sophia growls through gritted teeth. She slaps Lin lightly on the face. "We need to get outta here!"

To Sophia's relief—but also her disappointment—Lin's eyelids flutter. The woman moans and looks sideways at her.

"Idiot," she whispers faintly. "Why aren't you running?"

"You need to get up," says Sophia. "If you're gonna be the Empress of Time, you can't die in this field."

The faintest grin flutters over Lin's pale face. With an arm around Sophia for support, she struggles to her feet.

"I'll take the arrow out when we get to the farmhouse," Sophia promises. "But Redbeard is right. We'll stand more of a chance fighting them there than out in the open."

They trudge on, woman and girl, as hurriedly as they can under their circumstances. The sun disappears behind gray clouds, and a clinging, wet chill cloaks them. After what seems like forever, they turn up the farmhouse's gravel drive and through a rotting gate.

Lin's strength is fading into nothing when Sophia opens the creaky farmhouse door and drags her inside. Finding a dusty sofa, she lowers Lin gently onto her belly. Exhausted, Sophia wishes she could collapse too.

Not yet. Soon, maybe. But not yet.

Sophia hurries to the window and peers out. At least for the moment, no one appears to be following them.

Then, turning back to Lin's unconscious figure, she whispers, "And now for that arrow."

Chapter Nineteen

THE FINAL PIECE

"I CAN'T BELIEVE YOU'RE ALIVE."

Lin Lai's eyelids flutter. A filament of sunlight sneaks through the curtains and lands on her face.

"I can't believe I *saved* you."

"Do you mean you can't believe you were *able* to save me?" Lin asks weakly. "Or that you could *make* yourself save someone like me?"

"Both, I guess," Sophia replies. As she gazes down on the resting woman, she subconsciously covers her scarred wrist with her right hand. "Letting you die would've been the easy thing to do. But my dad always told me the easy thing isn't usually the right thing. So ... here we are."

Lin scoffs and turns away so she doesn't have to look at the girl. "If you knew what was good for you, you would have let me die," she whispers.

"Yeah, I know. But I wasn't thinking about what was good for *me*. I was thinking about what was *good*."

Lin chuckles derisively. Even after being rescued by Sophia, her voice is edged with spite. "Have you been rehearsing that line? Sitting there while I was asleep, thinking of all the things you might say to change me? To make me noble and virtuous and *good?* Like yourself?"

Sophia frowns. She sits on the sofa's arm and says, "No. Mostly I was spending my time saving your life."

That dampens Lin's spite. She glances around the dingy room and takes a deep breath of the clammy air.

"Did you fight them here too?" she asks.

Sophia shakes her head. "Nope. They never came."

"Redbeard?"

She hangs her head and shakes it again, slowly. "He didn't come either."

After an uncomfortable pause, Lin asks, "How did you get the arrow out?"

"It wasn't too hard. When I was cutting off your shirt, I noticed a weird bulge in your chest," Sophia explains. "I figured it had to be the arrowhead. So I shoved it the rest of the way through, snapped it off, and then pulled the rest out through your back. Easy as pie."

"Is there infection?" Lin asks the question timidly, afraid to hear the answer. An infection here would likely mean death.

Sophia answers, "You also got lucky with that. I found a whole bunch of antibiotics in the upstairs bathroom. I don't know if the owners were stashing them or what, but if you keep taking them, you shouldn't get an infection."

"Any damage to internal organs?" Lin asks.

"Don't know," Sophia mutters. "Sorry. I'm not a doctor. Can't be anything too severe, otherwise I don't think you'd be talking to me right now. But I wouldn't be surprised if you end up with some problems down the road."

"You know, that was very clever of you," Lin says, flashing Sophia the tiniest of grins.

"What was?"

"Hiding your pistol. I make a point never to underestimate an enemy, but clearly I made that mistake with you. I'm sorry you weren't able to use it the way you had planned."

Sophia plays dumb. "What do you mean?"

"To escape from *me*. You were waiting for the right moment to use it, when you could escape me for good."

"I still might, you know."

"Yet even now, you don't. Why?"

"I already told you why. Because helping someone when they're hurt is the right thing to do. Even a *bad* someone, like you."

"Then why didn't you use it when I took you from Ettore? I wasn't hurt then!"

Sophia gulps and stumbles for words. "Because—because I didn't know if I could grab it and fire it in time. You had the knife, and you were also driving, so if we crashed—"

"That," interrupts Lin, "is complete nonsense. My attention was fully on the road, and we weren't driving fast. If you had shot me then, you would have wound up in a ditch with nothing worse than a headache."

Sophia glares at her. She tries to summon the old defiance, but she feels Lin tearing down her walls like some psychological wrecking ball.

"You did not use it," Lin declares, "because you will not kill unless you are given no other choice. And eventually, in this world, that kind of goodness will be the death of you."

A long pause follows. There is nothing more to say.

Outside, a bank of gray clouds swallows up the sun. The shadows in the room darken.

Lin, with much wincing and gritting of teeth, pushes herself into a fully seated position.

"I'm not sure you should—" Sophia begins, but Lin cuts her off with a dismissive wave.

"My wound is what it is," she says. "It has cost me too much time already. Is there anything to eat here?"

"Not really. There was an unopened bag of chips in the pantry and a jar of pickles, but I already ate them."

"How long was I unconscious?" Lin asks.

"About a day. Little more."

The self-named Empress of Time stands so abruptly, she almost falls over again. Sophia grabs her arm to steady her.

"Wasted more time than I thought," mutters Lin, irritated. "Get your things—"

"I don't have any things."

"—and let's go. Have you been outside? Is there a car?" she asks, crouching to grab her backpack from the ground.

"There's a truck parked behind the house," Sophia answers, "and I already found the keys."

"Then come," Lin orders sternly. She doesn't sound like a woman whose life Sophia saved. "We must continue."

"Seriously?" Sophia replies. She can't believe what she's hearing. "Four of your people, maybe five, were just taken prisoner. Shouldn't you be going after *them*? Not some relic!"

In a small, distant voice, Lin says, "There must be sacrifices upon the path."

"Sacrifices?" says Sophia. "What path?"

"Never mind," retorts Lin. "It doesn't matter. They knew the danger they were putting themselves in by joining me. I would be dishonoring them if I *didn't* press on. Besides, we have no idea where they were taken or if they are still alive. I will not waste precious time searching for people who may never be found. Now, you may either come with me or rot here along with this farmhouse. Decide quickly."

Sophia fumes silently. Lin's near-death experience hasn't changed her at all. She's the same demanding, power-hungry villain she was yesterday.

But at present, Sophia doesn't have many options for companionship, so she sighs in defeat and says, "I guess I can't let you go alone. Plus, I need the relic just as much as you."

"That's the spirit," replies Lin. Then she adds, "But if you cross me and try taking the relic for yourself, it will be the last thing you ever do—gun or not. Do you understand?"

Although Sophia doesn't know if Lin can back up the threat, she nods and pulls the truck keys from her pocket. Behind the house, they find a teal pickup that appears to be half Ford, half rust.

"Can you drive?" asks Lin.

"Of course."

The engine roars to life at once. Sophia notices there isn't much fuel left in the tank, but she supposes it will be enough to bring them to the next town. She shifts the stick into gear, and the party of two rolls around the house and along the gravel drive. When they meet up with the main road, both peer back in the direction they came yesterday.

The two wrecked vehicles remain right where they left them. There is no sign of anyone near them, either living or dead.

"Drive us to our car," says Lin. "I want to see if they left anything."

Sophia does as told. She remains inside the truck while Lin examines the ruined vehicle.

Lin groans when she looks in the trunk. The raiders have pried it open and stripped it clean of anything useful. Her bow and quiver of arrows are gone.

She expected as much. Still, all is not lost. Yes, the bow is her favorite weapon, but her father also made certain she was well trained in many forms of hand-to-hand combat. Her knives will be plenty deadly for anyone foolish enough to stand in her way.

"There is nothing here," says Lin, returning to the pickup truck. "Let's go."

"What about the other car? And your people? Are you sure—"

Lin cuts her off. "No looking back. There is only forward. Turn us around."

Sophia sighs with disappointment but obeys. She should know by now that Lin won't budge.

But before they pass the farmhouse, Lin shouts, "Stop! Stop the truck!"

Sophia slams on the brakes, certain they are under attack again. Glancing around, she sees only empty land and lonesome road.

Lin raises a finger, pointing across the heath to a handful of low mounds.

They are bodies. Seven, maybe eight of them.

None are moving.

Sophia lets the truck idle, and both climb out. They cross the spongy turf, picking their way carefully across the uneven terrain.

As they approach, Sophia spots Redbeard's body lying among the rest.

"How did he manage to kill so many?" Sophia wonders aloud.

"Redbeard was a highly skilled soldier," Lin answers. "I know he may not have seemed the type, but he spent his entire adult life in a British special forces unit."

Sophia stays put while Lin picks her way through the bodies. She kneels at Redbeard's side and whispers something, but her murmurs are unintelligible to Sophia's ears. As she speaks, Lin strokes his face lightly with her fingers.

As if Redbeard's body has shot an electric current through her, she jumps to her feet.

"Sophia! Come quickly!" she yells.

Dodging the other corpses, Sophia hops and skips to Redbeard. She looks down at him. His clothes are ripped and tattered. Bloodstains, the roses of battle, have blossomed over much of his body.

Sophia feels nauseous. What sick reason did Lin have in wanting her to witness the carnage up close?

Then she sees it. Redbeard isn't entirely still and silent, as the dead are. There is a faint hiss coming from his lips, and his chest rises and falls.

He's alive. But barely, by the looks of him.

"Help me lift him," Lin commands. Though she herself is wounded and weak, she drops to her knees and wraps his arm around her shoulders. Seeing Sophia's hesitation, she yells, "Now!"

Trying her best to ignore the warm, sticky blood, Sophia positions herself beneath Redbeard's other arm. Straining, grunting, and sweating, they hoist his mostly dead weight off the springy tundra. They struggle mightily—and once even drop the injured man—but after ten exhausting minutes, they've successfully hauled Redbeard to the truck. In another five he is lying across the back seat with his knees bent into the air.

"What now?" Sophia asks, wheezing to catch her breath in the damp Icelandic air. "Do you have emergency equipment on the boat?"

"Some, but not much," Lin replies. For a long moment, she stares at her unconscious lackey. "We will stick to the plan and continue to the West Fjords. We will find supplies along the way to bandage his wounds."

"What?" cries Sophia. She can't believe Lin's insistence that they push forward with the plan. "Are you *that* crazy? He's gonna die if we don't get him real help!"

"And where do you plan on finding that help?" Lin snarls. "Stoker was our only medic, and not a very skilled one at that. Cook and Columbia aren't doctors. I'm not a doctor. And, unless you were lying earlier, neither are you."

The girl glares back silently.

"No? Okay. Then we will do the best we can with what we find on the road. So, you start driving, and I'll give him some of my antibiotics. If those wounds aren't infected already, they will be soon."

For once, Sophia has neither a logical nor moral response. She knows Redbeard would stand no better chance on the boat. Still, it feels wrong plowing ahead like this, going for the relic while a man's life hangs in the balance.

With no real options, Sophia drives northwest. Fearful of another attack, she keeps a cautious eye on their surroundings. They pass through a few tiny hamlets, but none looks like the kind of place they might find the medical supplies needed to help Redbeard.

An hour later they approach a crossroads with one lonely building. In front of it is a handmade sign written in English: "Petrol! Grocery! Camping Gear!"

Sophia pulls into the parking lot.

"What are you doing?" demands Lin, offended that Sophia would dare try anything without first being told.

"They have camping gear here," Sophia answers calmly, "and camping gear means first aid supplies. Trust me. Plus, they'll probably have things for tourists. Guidebooks, maps—stuff like that. Things that might help us find the relic. *And* we're almost out of gas. We need a different car. Enough reasons for you?"

This time it is Lin who has no response.

They leave Redbeard in the truck. Inside the store, Lin makes for the camping supplies, while Sophia searches behind the checkout desk. As she hoped, it doesn't take long to find a set of keys. One of them, she is certain, will fit the ignition in the Suzuki Jimny, a compact sporting vehicle she noticed parked alongside the building.

With one task finished, she starts toward Lin on the other side of the store. A rack of tourist pamphlets grabs her attention along the way, and she stops. Her eyes flit across them. Most advertise some kind of outdoor adventure company. "Climb a Glacier with *Ice Tours!*" "Explore the Rainbow Colors of Leiðarendi Lava Cave!" Sophia wonders how anyone could pronounce half the names she sees. "Visit the Bjargtangar Lighthouse at the Látrabjarg Bird Cliffs!"

Her eyes pass to the next pamphlet ... and suddenly dart back.

Something about the white lighthouse on the pamphlet's cover has jumpstarted an odd feeling inside her. She picks it up for a closer look. Near the bottom, a smaller second picture displays a puffin at rest from its flight. The black-and-white seabird is perched atop a high cliff, staring out at the sea over its multicolored beak.

When Sophia opens the pamphlet to read more, her heart leaps into her throat.

"Lin!" she cries, waving the pamphlet. "I think I found something. Do you have that poem? The one from the North Cape?"

Lin looks at her, puzzled over the girl's sudden excitement. Nevertheless, she recites from memory:

> *"Unmoving I am, yet moved on have I—*
> *The relic with me—where the cliff dwellers fly*
> *Gone back to the house that lights my heart best*
> *The most extreme point 'twixt the north and the west—"*

"Yes!" Sophia exclaims, cutting off the rest of the poem. "It's right here! At the lighthouse by the bird cliffs!"

Lin snatches the pamphlet, and her eyes widen. Aloud, she reads, "'Located in the Westfjords, this westernmost point of Iceland—and Europe—is home to the hundred-year-old Bjargtangar Lighthouse and the majestic Látrabjarg Bird Cliffs!' This must be it!"

For a moment, Lin Lai looks less like a ruthless megalomaniac and more like a giddy middle-school girl asked to the homecoming dance by the popular boy.

Reassuming her stony demeanor, Lin says, "Well done, Sophia. You have found the final piece of the puzzle. The only thing left to do is claim the relic as my own."

The fires of greed and desire have rekindled in her dark eyes. Without another word, Lin exits the store.

As Sophia watches her go, she wonders if she should have kept her mouth shut.

Chapter Twenty

WHERE THE CLIFF DWELLERS FLY

SOPHIA DRIVES NORTH WITH a growing sense of dread. Working in the cramped space behind her, Lin patches up Redbeard as best she can. They've lowered the back seat so that he can stretch comfortably across the floor there. For two hours they travel this way. When Lin can do nothing more for her friend—her *attendant*—she climbs into the passenger seat and buckles herself.

"It is up to him now," she says softly.

More and more, Sophia believes Lin Lai to be a creature of two at-war personalities. Most of the time she is fierce and unyielding, a hurricane in human form. Yet deep within the storm there is an eye, gentle and mild. Even serene, at times.

It's an unsettling combination.

When darkness blankets the island, Sophia assumes they will find someplace to stop for the night.

Lin has other ideas. "Keep driving while you can," she orders. "When you are too tired to go further, I will take over."

They reach the West Fjords sometime during the first hours of night. A ghostly half-moon sails lazily on tufts of high cloud. Its bright, silvery glow creates a grand spectacle among the fjords. Shimmering with a million moonbeams, the deep inlets are like icy fingers, reaching into the surrounding mountains, trying to pull them into the sea.

Sophia drives late into the night, until her eyelids no longer cooperate. She pulls over, switches places with Lin, and is asleep in a matter of moments.

She awakens hours later. The faint light of early morning surrounds them, as does a bank of fog so thick she can barely see the hood of the car. Lin is in the driver's seat, arms crossed and fast asleep.

Sophia checks on Redbeard. She expects to discover that he died during the night. It comes as a shock when she sees his eyes open and his mouth moving wordlessly.

She doesn't need to be a lip-reader to know what he wants. After grabbing her water bottle and uncapping it, she pours a few drops into his mouth. He works it around, swallows it, and opens up for more. They continue this way until Redbeard is satisfied.

"What—what happened?" he asks. His voice is strained and hoarse.

"We made it to the farmhouse, thanks to you," Sophia replies with a grateful grin. "Lin took an arrow, but she's doing alright. When we found you the next day, we thought you were dead. But Lin's been working hard to fix you up."

"It doesn't"—He stops to take a breath—"feel like I'm fixed."

Sophia looks him up and down, then says, "Well, you're still in pretty bad shape, to be honest. You killed so many of those Vikings— or whoever they were—but they got in a few good blows too."

"You are extremely lucky to be alive," Lin comments, awakened by their conversation. "We are as well. We owe that to you."

"Just doin' my duty, Empress," he whispers, closing his eyes. "My life for yours. That was part of the promise we made, remember?"

Lin stares through the windshield. For a moment, she keeps silent, then says, "Yes. I remember. You, Mouse, Stoker, Caesar, Q—you all have proven yourselves faithful."

The deep disgust rises again in Sophia's breast, like bile up from her stomach. What kind of person would force others to swear that kind of allegiance? Who would elevate her own life so much higher than those of her people? Surely only the greatest monsters of history ever did such a thing!

And Lin Lai, despite the mask of gentleness and gratitude she sometimes wears, stands among the worst of those monsters. Sophia is sure of it now. She will never let herself be seduced again. She will never consider the tiniest possibility that anything good could live inside the heart of Lin Lai.

"Where are we now?" Redbeard asks.

"Stuck in fog, unfortunately," Lin replies. "In the West Fjords. We are on our way to a lighthouse here. I am convinced it is where the Immovable has taken the relic."

"Good," he whispers. "Good."

With that last word trailing on his lips, Redbeard slips back into sleep. Or perhaps a coma. Sophia isn't sure she knows the difference.

"Time to go," Lin says, turning the key in the ignition. "Fog or not, we at least have daylight now."

Sophia closes her eyes as they traverse the winding fjords. Only when Lin tells her they have exited the fog does she open them again. As in much of the country, they pass through the tiniest of villages. Most consist of less than a dozen homes and a few other structures: docks, warehouses, garages, and the like. Vibrant green pastures, nestled in deep valleys between the mountains, contain scattered farmhouses and herds of sheep or horses.

Morning drags on. The clouds lift higher into the sky but remain just as gray. The travelers pass a sprawling white sand beach, which seems out of place on this island of dark, volcanic earth. After the beach, the road turns inland. They wind up a steep bank and over it, descending into another village.

Somehow, Sophia knows the trip is at its end. The deciding moment is at hand.

She wonders what this Immovable will be like. Man or woman? Tall, short, thin, fat? Crazy and violent, like the old guy who attacked Gabriel and almost murdered Sophia? Or wise and gentle, as she imagines the poem's writer might be? Her stomach is queasy and her mouth dry as she wonders whether she will have to fight again. And perhaps die.

They pass an old campground, and the road climbs along a rising cliff face. To the left are green and grassy hills. To the right, a steep drop into the sea. As they ascend the final stretch of hill, a lighthouse rises into view. First the top, then the whole thing.

There is a parking lot at the end of the road. As soon as they enter it, Lin whips the car around so that it is facing the direction they just came. For a split second, Sophia wonders whether the Empress of Time has caught a case of cold feet. But when Lin parks the Jimny, Sophia realizes she was simply positioning them for a quick getaway.

A dissonant chorus of seabirds fills Sophia's ears when she opens her door. Although they are all different shapes and sizes and species, they enjoy the stiff breeze together. They're free and happy as they soar and cartwheel and dive about the cliff, with neither care nor concern for the showdown about to take place.

"Would you mind opening the back hatch?" Redbeard asks, awake again. "I want to hear the birds. Smell the breeze."

Sophia fulfills the request, and he thanks her.

Lin, armed to the teeth with knives and other weaponry, approaches Sophia. "You have a choice," she says. "You may stay here with Redbeard, or you may come with me wherever this leads."

As always, the girl's curiosity, bravery, and sense of adventure outweigh her fears, so she answers, "I'm going with you. You might need me. So might the Immovable."

Side by side, they approach the lighthouse. It isn't the tall, tube-shaped structure Sophia imagines most lighthouses to be. This one is short and boxy and has certainly seen better days. Its white paint is chipped and peeling. The walls themselves are cracked and crumbling. One of its windowpanes is broken, replaced with plywood. The only part of the building that appears to be in good shape is the lantern room itself. The rounded, glass-walled room faces the sea, where for a hundred years it warned sailors away from the deadly rocks and cliffs.

"Do you really think anyone lives inside *that?*" Sophia asks as she appraises the shabby structure.

"Perhaps," Lin replies. "Or perhaps in that village we passed through."

The windows in front are too high for either of them to look inside. After walking once around the lighthouse and finding no other windows, Lin opts for the straightforward approach. With her metal-plated, gloved fist, she hammers on the door so hard, Sophia thinks she's trying to break it down.

"Open up!" Lin yells. "I have come for the relic, and I will not leave until it is mine! So come out of there!"

Nobody answers. Lin knocks again, but the result is the same.

Next, she tries beating down the door. She hammers it with her good shoulder and kicks her heel into the lock, but the door doesn't budge.

"Maybe they aren't here anymore," suggests Sophia. "Or maybe they died."

"I do not think so," Lin says, pointing at the concrete beneath them. "Those muddy footprints are too well defined. They would not last long in a place as wet and windy as this, which means they were made recently."

As Lin continues her assault on the door, Sophia meanders to the edge of the cliff. Like in the pamphlet she found at the tourist shop, a puffin sits there, surveying the sea. Even when Sophia is close enough to touch it, the puffin doesn't move. It merely eyes her with a sort of pleasant curiosity. Only when the girl reaches for it does the puffin finally leap from its resting place to sail away on the breeze.

From here, Sophia can see that the cliffs stretch for miles southeast of the lighthouse. The further along, the higher they rise, cutting a jagged line between earth and sea.

It is along this craggy edge where Sophia spots him. A solitary figure with a bushy beard and a walking stick.

And he's walking toward her.

Sophia freezes. Should she hide? Try to conceal their presence?

No. That would be wasted effort. The man must have noticed her staring at him by now.

Yet he doesn't change his pace. He doesn't appear hurried or threatened. He is simply enjoying a leisurely stroll on a pleasant morning.

Sophia knows she should alert Lin, yet she does not. There's something about the man that has already earned her trust, though she cannot say why. For several moments she weighs her options. Then, before she realizes what her legs are doing, she starts toward him.

"Good morning!" he calls cordially to her, when Sophia is near enough to hear him. He speaks with a thick Scandinavian accent. "I wondered if anyone would solve the riddles I left at the North Cape. I was beginning to grow worried I would die with my secrets." With a laugh, he adds, "Or that I would have to create another poem."

Now that he is closer, Sophia discerns his features more clearly. He does indeed have a thick beard, more gray than brown. She guesses his age is somewhere between sixty and seventy, although he still appears strong and healthy. His sharp eyes are the emerald green of a mountain lake, quick and clear, and they give Sophia the uncomfortable sense that he is reading her heart and mind.

"Good morning," she replies. Suddenly aware of how near the cliff she is, Sophia prays she hasn't misjudged the man.

"My name," he says, extending a calloused hand, "is Einar Sturluson."

Tattooed below his wrist is an image of the letter *I*. Just like the old man who almost killed her.

"I'm Sophia," she replies. She shakes his gentle hand, but seeing the tattoo has unnerved her.

His eyes flick toward the lighthouse, and he says, "There is much for us to discuss. Perhaps it would be best if we included your friend in our conversation."

Sophia snorts. "She's not my friend. Be careful around her. She's dangerous."

"And, until I have the pleasure of knowing you better, I shall assume the same of you," Einar replies with a bemused grin. He beckons her forward with an outstretched palm. "Shall we?"

Lin spies them approaching. She stands tall and undaunted in front of the lighthouse door. One hand she places on the hilt of her longest knife, while the other remains balled up in an angry fist. She scowls at Sophia, and when the girl is close, she yells, "Why didn't you alert me?"

"He just wants to talk," Sophia says. "He's not dangerous."

"That is not entirely true," disputes Einar. "I certainly am dangerous to the wrong people, just as a mother bear is dangerous when someone threatens her cubs. But you have no need for your weapons. Not yet, at least."

Lin relaxes her grip on the knife.

From his pocket, Einar produces a brass key. He holds it up to prove it isn't a weapon and, with the same grin and glimmer in his eyes, says, "It is teatime, I believe. Care to join me inside?"

Without waiting for an answer, he steps past Lin, unlocks the door, and enters the lighthouse.

Sophia responds to Lin's angry glare with an innocent shrug, then follows Einar.

For something called a lighthouse, it's awfully dark inside. As far as furniture goes, Einar has adopted a minimalist approach. A picnic table sits against the left wall. A gas stove and tea kettle on the tabletop are the only cookware Sophia sees. In the back corner is a small desk, which holds a dozen books, a notebook, and a couple pens. An easy chair and floor lamp occupy the other rear corner. A ladder leads to a rectangular platform some ten feet above them, where a mattress and blankets serve as Einar's bed.

"It isn't much," Einar admits as he ignites the gas stove, "but it is home now."

"Why did you come here?" Sophia asks. "Why did you leave the North Cape?"

"Two reasons," Einar replies. He produces a large water jug from underneath the picnic table. With it, he fills the kettle. "First, because this is where I was born and raised. That little village you passed at the bottom of the hill—that was home for me. Even when my family moved to the city, I always considered this home. It is my favorite place in the world. I knew if I was going to be alone for the rest of my life, I wanted to be here."

"And the other reason?" Lin asks coldly.

"Too many people snooping about the North Cape," Einar answers casually. "*French* snoopers, at that. I had to leave."

Motioning toward the benches on either side of the picnic table, he says, "Please, take a seat. I have waited a long time for visitors."

Sophia sits as directed.

Lin doesn't. She narrows her eyes and says, "We came for the—"

Einar cuts her off. There is a dark, disapproving look in his face as he snaps, "I know what you have come for, Lin Lai."

Sophia's jaw drops. She hasn't mentioned Lin's name. Neither did Lin herself. How could he know it already?

What Einar says next is so shocking, even Lin must sit when she hears it.

Addressing her with a mocking tone of false dignity, he adds, "O Empress of Time."

Chapter Twenty-One

IMMOVABLE

EVEN IF LIN WERE WITNESSING her parents risen from the dead, she wouldn't be more stunned than Einar's words have left her. Her mouth opens and closes without a sound, like a beached fish gasping for breath.

"Is that not what you wish to be called?" Einar asks, his eyes boring into her. "Is it not the goal you seek? That all might someday call you 'Empress of Time'?"

"How—how do you know me?" Lin stammers. It's the first time Sophia has seen her flustered like this.

"I know many things about you," says Einar. "I know that you were the daughter of Chinese ambassadors. I know your parents were murdered for crimes they did not commit. I know you have loved. I know you have lost that love. I know it is your goal to control time, and thus to control all of history—past, present, and future. The information most relevant to our meeting today, however, is this: I know you are an enemy."

"How can I be your enemy?" Lin replies. "We have never met."

"I did not say you were *my* enemy," says Einar. "Although, yes, indirectly you are. Even more importantly, you are the sworn enemy of the 'One Who Mends Time Again.'"

Lin's eyes narrow into slits. She remembers the phrase from the poem Einar left at the North Cape, and she does not care for it one bit. The one who wants to control time will never peacefully coexist with the one destined to fix it.

Sophia uses the pause in conversation to ask, "And who is he? Or she? The One Who Mends Time, I mean."

Einar replies, "That is an answer I cannot give, for I do not know his name, nor do I know what she looks like. You see, I do not even know if the One is a *he* or a *she!* There is only one person, another Immovable like myself, who knows the full story, who holds all of our knowledge. And she lives across oceans. All I can tell you is that the One Who Mends Time was written about long, long ago."

"So it's some kind of prophecy?" Sophia asks, hoping for clarification.

Einar shakes his head. "Not prophecy. *History.*"

"But how can that be?" Lin demands. "I am only twenty-seven years old!"

"Yes, you are," Einar agrees. "And yet, in another sense, much older."

"More riddles!" Lin shouts. She slams her fist on the table. "I am tired of your games. Give me answers!"

"You shall have them," Einar replies. "But only the ones I know, and only the ones I am entitled to give."

"Tell me about the relics," Lin demands, cutting straight to her important business.

"The relics are as ancient as humanity itself," Einar explains. "Where exactly they came from, I am not sure anybody knows. But in the earliest days, the Immovables understood the power they contained. Even individually, they have significant effects on the people around them. They make time unpredictable. But when they are brought together, as they were meant to be, their power can be controlled and used. We Immovables realized the danger this posed. Quite simply, this is too much power for one individual to possess." As he speaks the words, he peers meaningfully at Lin. "Perhaps we should have destroyed the relics altogether, and so also the Antikythera Device itself. But doing so, we feared, would create innumerable fractures in time and space. Besides this, the Immovables also believed that, someday, there would come a person who could fix time, and the relics must be preserved for that to happen. So instead of destroying them, we hid them."

"But if you want to keep the relics hidden, why put the Hallowed Vaults in places where there were lots of people?" Sophia asks. "Like Las Vegas and that museum on the North Cape?"

"That isn't how it was intended, originally," Einar answers. "There is a complicated history involved in this, but it would take too long to explain the whole thing, so I will give you the short answer. You see, when the relics were first dispersed, they *were* taken to isolated places. They could not be *too* isolated, however. Like anybody else, Immovables need food and shelter and the company of other people. Over time, isolated places often became more populated. Instead of trying in vain to keep people away from the Vaults, we decided to camouflage them. Hide them in plain sight, so to speak. The altar at the North Cape is one example. Nobody would ever suspect that, hidden beneath a room visited by thousands of people each year, there was a treasure of priceless worth. Thus, we could preserve the relics until the time came for Time itself to be fixed!"

"But—I mean—Time is broken? What do you mean? How?" stammers Sophia.

"Time is not what it was meant to be," Einar answers. "What it *used* to be. I do not know much more than that. What I *can* tell you is that all these rips in Time are not natural. The sudden disappearance of humanity a few years ago is not a natural product of the universe. Yet such things have been happening throughout history. The sudden disappearance of the Mayans from Central America, or the people of the Roanoke Colony who vanished without a trace—these are but two examples. Throughout history there are hundreds, possibly *thousands* of stories about people disappearing, never to be seen again."

"I heard it might have something to do with space-time being fractured by the Sun," Sophia says. "Was that wrong?"

"Perhaps not entirely," Einar replies. "Intense activity from something as large as our Sun could serve as a catalyst, disrupting an already agitated environment. Like when you have a pot of water or a tea-kettle"—He motions to the one in front of him—"on the cusp of boiling. Stir it with a fork or a spoon, and that tiny bit of extra energy can send it into a boil. Days before humanity disappeared, the head-lines were full of articles about solar flares larger than any we had seen before. So, yes, your theory does make some sense."

"Then why did so many of us slip forward to *this* time?" Sophia asks.

"What do you mean?" Einar inquires, puzzled.

"Me and Lin and our other friends—we all come from different places and different times. But when we slipped through time, we all ended up alone in November 2026. Why?"

Einar stares at the tabletop, considering her question. After a bit of thought, he says, "I am sorry. I do not know. My best guess is that when humankind slipped away and disappeared, some sort of vacuum or imbalance was created which pulled you in to fill it. Or at least to fill *part* of it. But it is only a guess."

"And why," asks Lin, "didn't you disappear along with everybody else? Why are you still here?"

"As I already mentioned," says Einar, "the relics, even by themselves, have tremendous influence on the people and environment around them. But there are certain people—and I am one of them—who are, for some reason, unaffected. Maybe it is something in our DNA. Maybe there is something supernatural behind it. I don't know. But we are completely unable to move through Time. We are *immovable*. We stay where we are—*when* we are—which makes us the best candidates for guarding the relics."

"Can I ask something else?" says Sophia. "The old man from the map room in Las Vegas tracked us down and tried to murder me and another boy. He was ready to kill us in order to stop us from finding the relics."

Einar frowns and says, "Poor Leroy. He was the best of us. A gentle and capable fellow, if you'll believe it. But the isolation must have been too much for him. Being alone for so long can do strange things to a person's mind."

"But why aren't you trying to stop us too?" asks Sophia. "Isn't that your job?"

Einar leans forward and narrows his eyes. His tone is deadly serious as he says, "Where did you get the idea that I will not try to stop you? The relic is for the One Who Mends Time, not for the one who seeks to make herself ruler over it. Once this conversation is over, I will suggest that both of you return to your car and drive away."

"That," Lin says darkly, "is not how this ends, Immovable."

The man stares at her, unblinking, as if trying to freeze her with his icy gaze. Then, curtly, he says, "There is one other thing I want to tell you, Lin Lai, Empress of Time. I want to share what our ancient histories tell us happens to you."

Lin returns his frosty gaze. She does not speak.

There is pure loathing in Einar's stare as he continues, saying, "They speak of a reckless woman who hurts everyone around her. A woman so consumed with power that in the end, she is swallowed up entirely. A woman who is given every opportunity to walk away from her path of self-destruction, yet makes all the wrong choices. Choices which seal her own doom."

Lin leaps up from her seat to tower over Einar. In that moment, she doesn't appear five-and-a-quarter feet tall. She is a wrathful giantess, ready to crush anyone who crosses her.

"My life will not be determined by your ancient myths," she tells him. There is an unsettling calmness in her voice. "I determine the outcome of my own story. And the next page of my story will go one of two ways: with your dead body at my feet, or with your relic in my hands."

Einar sighs wearily. "So, we come to it. The moment I saw you with the girl, I did not think it could be avoided."

The much older man stands. The kettle has just begun to whistle as he turns off the burner and says, "Teatime will have to wait. Come outside. We will do this behind the lighthouse. If I am about to die, I will do so with the vision of my cliffs in my eyes and the sound of my birds in my ears."

As he exits the lighthouse, he snatches his walking stick from beside the door. Lin and Sophia follow. The former already has a knife in her hand. Sophia is sure the only thing keeping her from stabbing him in the back is the relic. Lin needs to know where it is before she can kill him.

When they are all in front of the lighthouse, Einar faces Lin. "I assume you will be using your knives."

Lin nods.

"And I will use my staff," he announces, holding up his walking stick. "If you beat me in combat, I will hand over the relic to you. If I win—and if you are still alive—you will drive away, and you will let Sophia remain here with me. You will leave Iceland, leave your ambitions behind, and abandon your foolish quest to become Empress of Time. Agreed?"

"Agreed!" Lin shouts. In the very same moment, she lunges forward, trying to catch Einar off guard.

Sophia cries out, fearing the worst for him. He hasn't even raised his staff.

With the deftness of a much younger man, he twirls gracefully aside and out of Lin's path. As she hurtles past him, he smacks her stiffly behind the kneecaps with his walking stick. She stumbles forward and nearly onto her face.

Embarrassed, and red with rage, Lin whips around with a knife clenched in each fist. She comes at him again, slower this time and more methodical. She slices and stabs at the air. It looks again like she will surely skewer him with at least one blade, if not both. But before the knives reach him, Einar raises his staff so that it is parallel to the ground. He catches both blades on it at once, then thrusts the staff's rounded end between them and into the bridge of Lin's nose.

She curses as she drops both knives. Wiping a gush of blood from her nostrils, she retreats a few paces.

"Will you yield?" asks Einar, offering her an end to the duel.

Lin answers by unsheathing two more blades from her hip. These are longer, more like short swords than knives, curved and cruel. Each looks capable of chopping Einar's walking stick clean in half. She advances, thrusting and slashing madly, as if she believes rage itself will be enough to win the fight.

This time, Einar not only disarms her, but takes her all the way to the ground in the process. In a flash, Lin is flat on her back, panting to regain her breath. The point of Einar's staff is pressed against the base of her throat.

"All I have to do," he says, "is lean forward, and you will never breathe again. Will you yield now?"

With no other option, Lin nods.

"Throw your weapons aside," he orders.

Another half-dozen blades are soon scattered on the grass. Only then does Einar remove the staff from her throat.

He turns to give Sophia a wink. Her captivity—and Lin's reign of terror—have come to an end.

It is a tiny opportunity Einar gives her, but Lin takes advantage of it. Quick as a whip, she reaches to her ankle. The blade hidden there, unbeknownst to either Sophia or Einar, flashes in the light of the gray morning as she hurls it at the unsuspecting man.

Sophia shouts, trying to warn him.

She is almost successful.

Einar dives aside. The blade, intended for more vital organs, lodges itself into his upper arm. He screams in pain as he hits the ground.

Most unfortunately, he has lost his staff.

By the time Einar twists himself into a seated position, Lin has recovered one of her curved swords. She advances, a dark, satisfied sneer curling her upper lip.

"You yielded!" Einar cries, gritting his teeth against the pain. "We had an agreement!"

Lin shakes her head and says, "Fulfilling my destiny and becoming the Empress of Time is worth one or two—or a hundred—broken agreements. And now, it is time for you to meet *your* destiny. Relic or not!"

She raises the blade high. In a moment, her arm will drop, and the

deathblow will come. Einar closes his eyes, ready to accept his fate
with dignity.

"Stop it, Lin!" Sophia cries out at the top of her lungs.

Lin glances at her angrily. At once, her pale faces grows even paler,
and she lowers her sword.

The pistol in Sophia's trembling hand is aimed directly at her head.

"Let him go!" the girl shouts, jabbing the gun at Lin for emphasis.
"Let him go, or I'll do what I should have done before. I'll shoot you,
Lin!"

There is a brief pause. Then the wicked grin curls Lin's lip again,
and she says, "No, I do not think so. You see, I know you, Sophia. You
are the girl who will not kill unless she has no other choice. You are
the girl who is too weak to do what must be done. But if you are going
to shoot me, you had better do it. I have had enough of this man and
his riddles."

For a moment longer, Sophia holds the gun level with Lin's head.
Then her eyes drop, and the pistol falls limply to her side. She turns
away, defeated and helpless.

"If you kill me," Einar says in his own defense, "you will never find
your relic. You will search and search for a hundred years, but it will
never be yours."

Leaning toward him, Lin growls, "I will rip apart your lighthouse
piece by piece. It may take some time, but I will find it."

"Do you truly think I would hide it there?" Einar asks. "Do you
think I keep it under my pillow, like a little girl's diary? Look around
you, Lin! There are miles of cliffs and hills here. How long do you
think it will take you to search all this?"

Lin frowns. She glances around, then lowers the blade.

"Let me live, and the relic is yours," he says. "I would gladly die
and take the secret to the grave with me, if it meant keeping your

hands off it. Unfortunately, I am not permitted to willingly let the relic's whereabouts die with me. It cannot be lost. So, congratulations, Empress. You win."

"And what's to stop me from killing you once I have the relic?" asks Lin.

"A fair question," replies Einar. "You have already shown me that your word is as valuable as puffin droppings. But there is one thing you don't know about me. Before I was recruited to be an Immovable, I was a doctor. A surgeon, in fact."

"And how will that save you?"

"It won't. Unless you also want to save the life of your friend. The one in the back of your vehicle. The one covered in blood."

Lin's eyes narrow as she considers his offer.

"Everybody lives," Einar says, "including your friend. And you walk away with the relic."

Lin nods. "Agreed."

She slides her sword back into its sheath. As if to demonstrate her control even further, she picks up Einar's staff and hurls it over the edge of the cliff.

He struggles to his feet, wincing with pain and grabbing at the blade in his arm.

"My apologies! I wouldn't want to forget this!" Lin exclaims cruelly, before yanking the knife from his shoulder.

Einar howls in agony. With his uninjured limb, he presses down on the wound, trying desperately to stem the flow of blood.

Lin wipes the bloody blade against her pants, then sheaths it at her side.

"I do hope I didn't hit any major arteries," she taunts. "You had better hurry to that relic. The sooner I have it, the sooner you can patch yourself up."

Turning to Sophia, she says, "You stay here with Redbeard. As soon as I return with the relic, we will hand him over to the care of this supposed surgeon. Then you and I are leaving."

"You're not gonna wait for him to get better?" Sophia asks incredulously. Once again, Lin's inhumanity seems to know no bounds. "You're going to abandon him here too?"

A wave of genuine regret washes over Lin's face as she says, "It may be weeks or months before Redbeard has recovered enough to travel. By then it will be winter, and we would be stuck here." She pauses and sighs. "The relics will not wait, so neither can we."

Lin's moment of hesitation ends as soon as it begins. She sets her jaw with cold and steely resolve as she viciously shoves Einar's injured shoulder.

"Lead the way, old man."

Chapter Twenty-Two

UPON THE BLACK SAND

A MISTY DRIZZLE HAS BEEN falling for the last hour. One of the car's riders is as gloomy and miserable as the weather outside. The other can't wipe the grin off her face. She is finally fulfilling her self-appointed purpose. She feels energized and confident, even giddy with victory. Her prize, at long last, is safely tucked away in her backpack beside the Book of Relics. There it waits to join the rest of its long-lost companions, the various pieces of the Antikythera Device.

Sophia says nothing as she stares out her window. Iceland is beautiful, but she wishes she could see the sun. She hopes the next relic is hidden somewhere a bit brighter.

She also wishes she could've had more time with Einar. There were a hundred questions she wanted to ask, and she has thought of a hundred more since they started driving.

How could Lin be both young and old? Ancient history, if she lives in the present? How can they protect themselves from the relic's unpredictability? Won't they be in danger of being thrown forward in time—or backward—simply by traveling with it?

Be patient. Keep your eyes, ears, and heart open. You will discover what you need.

Those were Einar's final riddling words to Sophia before she climbed into the car and left. She must hold them near to her heart as her journey continues. She must have faith that the road ahead will hold the answers she seeks, because she has no other choice.

"There is still an opportunity for you," Lin tells her that evening.

The rain has stopped, and the yacht is visible ahead, bobbing off-shore. The beach where they left the Zodiac is now only a few miles down the road.

"An opportunity for what?" Sophia asks miserably. She hasn't felt this depressed since her first days alone in the new world.

"To join me as I fulfill my destiny," answers Lin. "I was sincere when I said I wanted you at my side. There can only be one Empress of Time, but you could be my right hand. You are brave, smart, capable. You could take the place Ettore abandoned. Just think about it!"

Sophia shakes her head. "I don't need to think about it. I'll *never* think about it. I might be your prisoner, but I'll never be your partner."

"Then you are a fool," Lin says. "A fool who will die in the end."

Sophia sighs and says, "Maybe. But at least I'll be a fool who dies with her soul."

When they arrive at the beach, they park and exit the car. Lin grabs the backpack from behind her seat and leads the way down the black sand to the water's edge.

But as they approach the Zodiac, both realize there is a problem.

"What is this?" Lin shrieks, the rage boiling up and out of her. "How did this happen?"

The inflatable watercraft has been ripped to shreds. From its pontoons to its seats, anything that used to hold air can do so no longer.

"How are we supposed to get back to the boat?" Sophia asks, staring out over the water.

Then, as if answering her question—or challenging it—a flash of light engulfs the yacht. A rich *BOOM!* like a cannon blast bursts against her eardrums, followed by a low, ferocious rumble.

Lin screams with a fury unlike anything Sophia has heard before.

The yacht, floating lazily in the waves only moments earlier, has been swallowed in the flames of a massive explosion. Already, a plume of thick, oily smoke rises heavenward.

Sophia turns to find Lin standing statue still, a single tear rolling down each cheek. Despair and rage are mingled together in her eyes.

The girl realizes why. Not only has Lin lost her ride away from the island—she could always find another boat—but she has also lost all her people. Columbia and Cook, the last two, were waiting onboard for the return of their Empress. Now their remains are either swirling upward with the smoke or sinking into the ocean with the rest of the ship.

Sophia is about to say something, to offer some kind of sympathy, but the words catch in her throat.

"Lin," she whispers with alarm. "Turn around!"

Surrounding them, like phantoms in the twilight, are five figures. Together, they form a half-moon shape, tightening as they close in on Sophia and Lin.

They are completely cut off from the car. They can't even make a break down the beach without a fight. Outnumbered and pinned against the sea, surrender is their only option.

Without warning, Lin yanks Sophia roughly by the shoulder. She locks her arm around the girl's throat, pinning Sophia against her own body. With her free hand, Lin seizes the pistol from Sophia's hip holster and presses its muzzle against the girl's temple.

Sophia is so surprised, she hardly has time to cry out before Lin yells, "I warned you, Ettore! I warned you what would happen if you followed me!"

Sophia squints for a better look at the dark figures. In a moment, her heart rises from the darkness of terror into the light of radiant joy.

They have come for her. Her friends have come for her.

Kira and Kylah make up the left flank of the encroaching semi-circle, Dario and little Gabriel the right.

Ettore, the leader who brought them here, walks ahead of the rest.

The only ones not present are Micah and Bixby. Despite Sophia's joy, there is a resurgent wave of sadness as she remembers their lifeless bodies on the floor of the North Cape Hall. She realizes then that they never left.

But there will be time for tears and grieving later. Now is the moment of reckoning.

It begins with Ettore. The sound of his gentle voice cheers Sophia's heart as he says, "What then, Lin? What will you do after you kill her? Do you think you can gun us all down as well?" He shakes his head. "There is only one escape for you now. Let her go, and you will receive the same courtesy from us. As will your friends. I believe you call them Columbia and Cook."

"They are alive?" Lin asks. "How do I know you aren't lying?"

"I suppose you don't," replies Ettore. "You will have to trust that I am telling the truth. Between the two of us, I believe my word is the more trustworthy."

"Trustworthy?" Lin sneers. "How dare you lecture me on what it means to be trustworthy!"

Now addressing the rest of Ettore's crew, she asks, "Has your trustworthy leader shown you what he carries around in that suitcase? Has he? Maybe you should ask him! And has the most *trustworthy* Ettore told you about his past? Did he tell you how he came to be such a renowned physicist? Or how he came to know so much about the Antikythera Device, even *before* we broke into the Vatican Library together?"

"Lin, please—" Ettore begins calmly, but he is cut off.

"If you were so trustworthy," cries Lin, "you would not have abandoned me the way you did! If you were so trustworthy, you would not have stolen all the research we did together, leaving in the middle of the night without so much as a goodbye kiss! If you were truly trustworthy, you would have lived up to at least *one* of your promises to me! If you were trustworthy, you would still be at my side, just as you said you always would be!"

Ettore lowers his head, ashamed. Quietly, he says, "I could not follow you down that path any longer. I admit that the desire for power got the better of me. But only for a time. Then your mind and heart grew darker. Or perhaps that is how they always were, and I merely began to see the truth."

"But you promised me!" Lin screams, her voice sputtering and cracking with deep emotion. "You *promised* me."

"Yes," Ettore replies. "But you must learn, Lin, that only a fool will continue doing what he knows is wrong. No matter what promises he's made."

Lin's sobs tremble against Sophia's back. Suddenly, the girl is very afraid for her life. If Lin can do terrible things when she is calm and calculated, what damage might she cause when whipped into such an emotional state?

Ettore breaks away from the semicircle. He steps forward and says,

"Listen to me, Lin. I have Columbia and Cook tied up nearby. One of my people is guarding them."

A flutter of hope stirs in Sophia's breast. Who else could this be but Micah?

"If you kill Sophia," Ettore continues, "Dario will radio the guard, and Columbia and Cook will die. But if you let Sophia live—if you let her go—I will release them at once."

The ensuing pause lasts only a few seconds. To Sophia, it feels like an hour. Then Lin relaxes her hold on the girl's throat and pushes her toward Ettore.

Wrapping her arms around his waist, Sophia buries her face in Ettore's suitcoat. She knows she can't hold on forever, but she wishes she could.

He squeezes her briefly and whispers, "Behind me now, Sophia. This isn't over yet."

Sophia scurries across the black sand to Gabriel. As if she just found her own lost brother, she gathers him up in her arms and presses his freckled cheek against her own. She is powerless to restrain her joyful tears any longer as she whispers, "I was scared I'd never see you again."

"I wasn't," Gabriel replies, "because Micah told me the bad guys never win."

Sophia laughs aloud. Her joy over hearing Micah's name on Gabriel's lips could not be more complete—not unless Bixby himself came trotting down the beach.

"No, they don't," she whispers. She lets go of him and looks lovingly down into his almond-colored eyes. "Not today, at least."

Remembering the tense standoff happening behind her, Sophia returns her attention to the lovers-turned-enemies.

"Thank you, Lin," says Ettore. His words are heartfelt. "And now, for my end of the bargain."

He nods at Dario, who unclips a walkie-talkie from his belt.

"Cut them loose and send them back to the beach," Dario orders into the two-way radio. "Lin will be waiting here for them."

Ettore approaches Lin until he is standing within arm's reach. Without breaking his gaze from hers, he extends a hand, palm upward.

"I also need the gun, Lin," he calmly demands.

"You can have it," she replies with a cold snarl, "but only after I have used it."

Ettore furrows his brow, perplexed at what she might mean.

"I said I would let Sophia live," Lin explains. "But I said nothing about *you*."

Ettore cries out in horror. He realizes her murderous intentions, but too late.

Lin raises the pistol to his forehead and, amid a chaotic chorus of shouting, pulls the trigger.

Nothing happens.

She squeezes the trigger a second time, and then a third, but a harmless *click* is the only sound the pistol produces.

"I probably should have told you," Sophia says, grinning slyly as she strolls toward Lin. "There aren't any bullets left. I used them to fend off the Vikings. Every. Last. One."

"But then, when we were at the cliffs—"

Sophia cuts her off. "That's right. I didn't have any bullets then, either. If I did, do you really think I would have backed down? I would have shot you a hundred times before I let you hurt Einar."

Lin falls into a seething silence. She knows she has lost.

Holding out her open hand, Sophia says, "I'll take my pistol now."

Defeated, Lin places the gun into her outstretched palm.

"*And* we'll take the backpack," Sophia adds.

Upon hearing this, Lin backs away, searching furiously for an exit. But there is none. Only the cold sea behind her, and her enemies in front.

"I will never forgive this," Lin hisses, slipping the backpack's straps from her shoulders. "The next time I see you, I will kill you with my bare hands."

Sophia takes the backpack and replies, "*If* you see me again. And *if* that happens, I'll be ready for you. Until then, good luck. Go find your friends. I know you've given up on them, but they still might be alive. And think about what Einar told you. About your choices. You can always take a different road."

With that, Sophia Faraday takes one last look at Lin Lai and rejoins her friends.

"Wait here for Columbia and Cook," Ettore instructs Lin. "Then go, find somewhere to live out your life in peace. I beg it of you."

Lin doesn't reply. Angry tears glisten in her eyes as she turns and sits and stares out at the darkening sea.

"This world has so much to give you," Ettore whispers. There is an unmistakable look of longing in his face as he adds, "Be content with that."

Then he, too, turns up the beach, leaving the Empress of Time to fume upon the black sand, backpackless and utterly alone.

Chapter Twenty-Three

THE NEXT PAGE

THE OLD FISHING BOAT isn't a tenth as nice as the yacht. Rust has overtaken most of its paint, and everyone shares cramped bunk-rooms. The entire vessel creaks each time they encounter a large swell in the water. And even if she closes her eyes to pretend she is on a luxury cruise, she still can't escape the funky smell.

But, despite all its problems, the floating rust-bucket is heaven on earth for Sophia Faraday. It is her home, because from now on, home will be wherever her friends are.

Upon the main deck, she stares over the railing at the endless sea. There isn't a cloud in the sky, and the morning sun showers her with warmth and light. As the salty breeze plays with her hair, she thinks back on the past evening—not what happened at the beach with Lin, but the things that happened *after*. She thinks of how she laughed and cried when they picked up Micah a half-mile down the road. He had, of course, been Ettore's mysterious "man" guarding Columbia and Cook, armed only with the pair of scissors he used to cut them free. Afterward, she listened with delight as Micah told the tale of their wild flight from Norway to Iceland. Dario, whose sole experience piloting a plane had been with Sophia, "turned everyone religious" as they prayed for their lives.

But the best moment of all came when she stepped onto the boat. There she was tackled by seventy pounds of jumping, licking, tail-wagging Bixby.

"We thought he was dying after the North Cape," Kylah told her. "Then we realized he was just depressed without you."

Bixby hasn't left her side since. Even now he sits beside her, nose poked through the bars of the railing to sniff the briny breeze. Sophia lazily trails her fingers along his head, and he gives them a single, loving lick.

"Feels like a lifetime ago, doesn't it?" a voice asks. Micah leans against the railing next to her, holding out a granola bar in foil wrapping. "You hungry?"

Sophia takes and opens it. She is already chewing her first bite when she remembers her manners and says, "Thanks. I've barely had anything to eat the last couple days." She swallows and asks, "But what did you mean? What feels like a lifetime ago?"

"Since we all met in Vegas," he explains. "It's only been a few weeks, but doesn't it feel like so much longer?"

Sophia thinks back. She remembers how afraid she'd been. She remembers hating Micah after he snatched her pistol outside the map room. She remembers how worried she was that they wouldn't let her get Bixby, that he would die alone in her motorhome. She remembers her midnight talk under the stars with Ettore, when he taught her about space and time and his theories about the Sun causing all their problems. She shudders to think again about the wild-haired man— Leroy, according to Einar—and how Micah saved her life.

He's right. It does seem like a lifetime ago.

"Maybe that's because life has changed so much," she replies. "You know, when I first slipped forward, there were a few months when I thought life would never be good again. But I was wrong. Even on the bad days, life is worth everything. Because as long as we're alive, it means we have hope, and beauty, and meaning. And knowing there are people to share those things with? Well, that just makes the bright things even brighter."

"Well said, Soph." The smile on Micah's face radiates pure joy. "Well said."

A long silence ensues as they gaze into the infinite blue of sea and sky, but it isn't awkward. Words aren't always necessary between friends.

"So, what now?" Sophia asks, finally breaking the comfortable silence. "What's next?"

"Relic number two, I'm guessing," Micah replies. "Actually, Ettore said he wants to meet with everyone about that. Says he's got some things to explain." He glances at his wristwatch. "Everyone's supposed to be in the mess hall in five minutes. But before I go, I was wondering if you could finish your story."

"Story?" she asks, befuddled. "What story?"

"The one about the old woman," he answers. "The one you told me on the plane. It's been buggin' me so much. I know you killed her. But you never said *how*."

For some reason, Sophia doesn't feel threatened by the memory anymore. A vision of Eleanor wafts in front of her mind's eye, but now she is just another phantom. She can't hurt Sophia.

"The pistol," she answers. "I was duct-taped to the chair, but only my arms. I could use my legs, so I was able to move around the room with it. Slowly, but I could. I could even get up the stairs. It was dangerous with the heavy chair attached to me, but I could do it. What I *couldn't* do was get through the basement door. She kept it locked. Anyway, I spent all night using my feet to open her cabinets and bins, looking for anything that could help get me free. Then I found it. The pistol. It was tough, but I grabbed it with my feet and managed to lift it up to my hand. I positioned myself so I could point it right at the bottom of the stairs, then started shouting like something was wrong. She hurried down to check on me and left the basement door open, just like I was hoping she'd do. When she reached the bottom of the stairs, I shot her. Twice. She died right there. After that I hauled myself upstairs, found a kitchen knife, and used my mouth to cut myself free. And ... that's it."

"The scars," he murmurs, nodding toward her wrist.

Without breaking her gaze from the ocean, the girl nods grimly.

"Sophia Faraday," Micah announces, "you are, without a doubt, the most incredible girl I've ever met. I'm glad we're on the same side, because I'd be terrified if we weren't."

"I'm glad too," she replies, unable to hide her delighted smile.

"Well, I gotta hit the john before our meeting," says Micah, backing away from the railing. "I'll see ya in the mess hall."

Micah leaves, and Sophia is alone with her thoughts once more. She could spend these minutes wondering about a million unanswered questions. She could wonder about the distant shores where her journey might bring her. She could wonder what other people, whether friend or foe, she might meet along the way. She could wonder about the fate of Lin Lai and whether the Empress of Time will meet up with them again. She could wonder about all the mysteries and riddles Einar left cluttering her brain. She could wonder what it will be like to see her family again, after they have all the relics and can reassemble the Antikythera Device.

But she doesn't want to wonder about the future any longer. Nor does she want to dwell on the past. She wants to fill herself with the present.

Because the present is where her friends are. Her new family. And they are more than enough.

Sophia turns away from the ocean and meanders to the mess hall. The windowless room's grimy walls and offensive odor fit right in with the rest of the ship. Everyone else is already there, so she sits in the cleanest seat she can find and gives Ettore her attention.

The tailored physicist stands in front of them. As always when at sea, he looks a little green, like he might lose his breakfast at any moment. On the floor by his feet are his briefcase and Lin's backpack.

"Thank you for joining me," Ettore greets them. "I hope you enjoyed a well-deserved rest last night."

"Not much, thanks," Dario replies, scowling. "Micah's snoring could wake the dead."

"Keep talkin' like that, and you might find out," threatens Micah, though his tone is empty of any real hostility.

Ettore ignores their bickering and continues.

"After what happened last night on the beach," he says, "there are some things I think I should tell you, and some things I should show you. Some are things of which I am deeply ashamed. I thought by keeping them secret, I could rewrite my past. But I was wrong. I realize now that I must *own* my past. In doing so, I can live a more honest present."

Everyone stares at him with rapt attention.

Ettore sighs deeply, then says, "I am a fraud. Even worse, I am a thief."

"Whaddya mean?" asks Micah.

"I mean many things," Ettore replies. "It goes all the way back to my career as a physicist. I received awards and international renown for the work I did. Even after I disappeared, books were written about my theories and discoveries. Yes, I was an accomplished physicist. But I was not the *brilliant* one everyone thought I was. Much of my work I stole from lesser-known but much more brilliant men and women than myself. What I was truly brilliant at was blackmail, and whenever one of them threatened to expose me, I would use whatever leverage I had to keep them quiet. I was young. As many young people do, I valued success and fame over the truly nobler things like integrity, honesty, and decency.

"It was my lust for fame and influence which ultimately led me to my great act of thievery. I was speaking one day to an archaeologist friend of mine, who was studying an ancient artifact found at the bottom of the ocean. They called it the *Antikythera Mechanism*."

Upon hearing this, the members of Ettore's crew glance with surprise at one another. Kira and Kylah mumble back and forth.

"Of course, the one he was studying was corroded from years spent on the sea floor. He told me, however, that one day a few Vatican officials came to study it in private. Naturally, he found it odd that men of the church would be so interested in what was essentially an ancient set of gears. As they were leaving, he overheard parts of their conversation. They spoke of his Antikythera Mechanism as being no threat. They said it could never work in the time machine, and that theirs, stored safely in the Vatican's archives, was still the only working piece of its kind."

"So you broke into the Vatican," Sophia says, quite matter-of-factly. "That's why you already had the suitcase when Lin first met you in Rome. You were planning to return to the library. You knew you could learn more about the Antikythera Device, because you'd already been there once before. When you stole their Mechanism."

Ettore hangs his head and says, "Yes. All the way back in 1938. I stole the Mechanism and was on the run when I slipped forward to the present. Then I knew it would be safe to return to the Vatican and learn as much as I could about the Antikythera Device—the time machine. I was returning to do exactly that when I met Lin. And from there, I believe you know the main details of the rest of the story."

He swallows and stares into the corner. For a moment, he is lost for words. Then he says, "I have had the Mechanism this whole time, here in my suitcase. I told myself the reason I could not show you was because I did not fully trust you. But Lin is right. I was the untrustworthy one. I see now that the true reason I hid it from you is because I was ashamed. Ashamed of my own dark secrets. Ashamed that if I showed you, I would also have to tell you the repulsive methods by which I acquired it."

Ettore takes a nervous sip of coffee from his mug. He is unable to look anyone in the eye as he says, "But that is who I *was*. It is not who I am today. I closed that book long ago, and today I want to start on a new page with all of you."

He glances from one member of his crew to the next. His eyes are searching them for some kind of reaction, whether it be hatred or pity or understanding—or even forgiveness.

Kylah breaks the silence. "Well? Can we see it? The Mechanism? I mean, you've got it right there in the suitcase, don't you?"

Ettore grins and nods. He picks it up and places it on the nearest table.

"This suitcase," he informs them, "is one I designed myself. There is a thin layer of lead and titanium alloy coating the entire interior. I believe it helps contain the relics' unpredictable effects on time. So far, at least, there have been no incidents—so long as the suitcase is latched and sealed."

"We don't need a science lesson!" exclaims Micah. "Just open it, will ya?"

Ettore undoes the clasps, opens the suitcase, and steps back. Everyone crowds around to gaze at what's inside.

There are two things. The first looks like it is made entirely of burnished bronze. Dozens of gears and wheels, all different sizes, are interlocked upon a flat, inch-thick slab of bronze. There are also finely etched numbers and words, both on the bronze sheet and even on the gears themselves. The whole thing seems to radiate some kind of mysterious energy, filling the air around it with an electric crackle and hum.

It is the Antikythera Mechanism.

"That," explains Ettore, "is the control panel for the entire machine. Unfortunately, I have no idea how to use it. By the time we have the other relics, perhaps I will have it figured out."

The other item in the suitcase is a cylinder, one foot long and four inches in diameter. It reminds Sophia of the canisters in the drive-through lanes at her parents' bank. Unlike the bronze device, the cylinder looks to be made mostly of glass and steel—or some other silvery metal. At the bottom of the cylinder, there is a small, circular protrusion, which looks like it may be used to connect with something else. But the strangest thing about the cylinder is the pulsing, ghostly blue light emanating from its center.

"What's this called?" Gabriel asks. Being smaller than everyone else, he has climbed onto the table for a better look inside the suitcase.

"It is the relic from the North Cape," Ettore answers. "The one we took yesterday from Lin. This is the Antikythera Battery."

"How do you know what it's called?" Kira asks.

"Because we took something else from her too," says Ettore, bending to pick up the backpack. From it, he removes a leather-bound sheaf of yellowing paper. "Ladies and gentlemen, I give you the Book of Relics."

At this there are whoops of cheering.

"Well, what's it say?" Kylah asks, unable to contain her excitement. "Where are we going next?"

"Let's close the suitcase first," Ettore replies, "and then we will look. Together."

When the suitcase is shut, latched, and safe on the floor, Ettore lays the Book of Relics flat on the table. Respecting its old age, he gingerly opens it to the middle.

Everything inside is written in black ink and by hand. On top of the left-hand page, in bold print, is that stretched-out *E* that Sophia recognized as half of the Greek letter *theta*. Below it is a sketch of the same cylindrical relic now in Ettore's suitcase. And, at the bottom of the page, the relic is given a name: *The Battery*.

On the right-hand page is an eight-line poem.

Sophia reads it and cannot keep herself from laughing. It would have led them directly to the hidden room below the altar.

"Are you ready for me to turn the page?" Ettore asks them. He is building the suspense as a parent might do with their children's Christmas presents.

"Yes!" they all shout at once.

Ettore turns the brittle paper gently to the next page. Every eye stares down at it.

All except two. Sophia isn't looking at the book. Instead, her eyes wander among the people gathered around it.

She smiles.

Gabriel notices and beams back at her. They don't share a word, because each already knows what the other is thinking.

Three weeks ago, they were two kids, alone in the vastness of an empty world.

Not anymore.

Wherever they go from here, at the very least, they will have each other.

They will never have to be alone again.

Chapter Twenty-Four

WHAT HAPPENED AT THE TEMPLE

A GOLDEN THREAD OF SUNLIGHT squeezes through the solitary crack in the stone wall and falls upon Itzel's closed eyelid. The eye beneath quivers back and forth, struggling between a dream and the waking world.

Suddenly, both the raven-haired girl's eyes burst open. She sits upright on her mat and glances around the room.

The dream was a lie. Her family is still gone. Only little Aapo is there, snoring softly and lying on the mat her brother once used.

A low growl rumbles through her stomach, and she wonders where they will find food today. For months they have been scavengers, going from home to home in Tikal with the hope of finding unspoiled food. Some days they eat well. Other days—most days—they go hungry. The fruits and vegetables have long since rotted away. Most of the dried grains they find are riddled with bugs. On a good day they will happen upon an unlucky turkey or guinea pig, but most of the animals have wandered off or been killed by predators.

Three months. It has been three months since their families, friends, and the entire population of Tikal disappeared. She and Aapo have searched for clues, have tried desperately to learn where everyone went.

But they have found nothing. It's as if thousands of people truly did vanish into thin air.

Itzel decides she will let Aapo sleep a while longer, so she creeps silently from the bedroom. She splashes water from a pitcher onto her face, then takes a long, refreshing drink. Outside, she sits on Grandmother Xoc's favorite chair. Staring at the fruitless avocado grove at the clearing's edge, she begins running through the list of today's tasks.

Obviously, finding food is their top priority. There are also leaks in the roof they must repair, water from the stream they must collect and sanitize by boiling, and clothes that need mending or replacing. She must also tend to her failing garden and work on the fences she is building for the wild pigs she snares in the jungle.

It will be a busy day. To Itzel, that is good. The busy days help distract her from the hunger and sorrow.

If only they could see me now, Itzel thinks with amusement. *No one would be calling me "lazy little Itzel" anymore.*

She allows herself another minute of rest. The peace of the morning is her favorite time of day. After this there will be chores upon chores until nightfall.

When her minute is over, she stands to wake Aapo. But as she turns toward the house, she freezes.

A man, old and bent and wearing a priestly robe, stands at the edge of the clearing. He is staring at her from the end of the jungle path. Itzel is sure she has never seen him in Cuzacal before, yet there is something familiar about him. Perhaps she met him once upon a time in Tikal?

He approaches her, making no sound as he walks. Nothing about his appearance seems threatening to Itzel, but she remains on her guard anyway.

"Good morning, old one," she says respectfully when he stops in front of her.

"Good morning to you," he replies, "Itzel of Cuzacal."

The girl is speechless. She doesn't know this man, yet he obviously knows her.

"Are you from Tikal?" she asks.

The old man nods. "The last one, I thought. Then I saw you and the boy yesterday."

"He is named Aapo," Itzel informs him. "We go to the city every day, hoping to find food. Please, forgive me for asking, but how do you know me? Have we met before?"

"Long ago, when you were very small," he answers.

"I am much bigger now," Itzel says. "How did you know I was the same person?"

"Because," he says, his gray eyes piercing and clear, "you look so much like my own daughter. Your mother."

It takes a moment for the full meaning of the old man's words to sink in. When they do, Itzel breathlessly replies, *"Mam?* Grandfather?"

The old man nods, slowly and silently.

"They told me you were dead," says Itzel, feeling both confused and a little betrayed.

"Not truly dead, though to our family I was as good as such," he replies cryptically. "I was given a job of highest honor, but it meant I could be part of my family no more."

"Then why are you here now?" Itzel asks.

"Forgive me," her grandfather says, "but I am old and cannot stay far from my place of rest for long. I must return to Tikal."

"Already? Why?" Itzel asks, frustrated.

When her grandfather grins at her, his brown face crinkles with a thousand new wrinkles. He says, "I do not mean to leave you. I would like for you and the boy to accompany me back to Tikal. There, I will explain everything."

Without hesitation, Itzel runs into the hut and awakens Aapo. The boy is rubbing the sleep from his eyes when he steps outside, and he squints against the morning sun.

The old man is gone. Itzel's heart drops like a stone before she realizes that he is already on the jungle path, his ancient legs shuffling toward Tikal.

"Who is that?" whispers Aapo. "Where did he come from?"

"He is *nimam,* my grandfather," answers Itzel. The words feel strange on her tongue. "He says he is from Tikal."

"Tikal!" Aapo shouts with disbelief. "If he is from Tikal, how have we not seen him yet?"

"I do not know," says Itzel, shaking her head. "He says he will explain everything to us, if only we follow him."

It doesn't take long to catch up. Once they do, they walk slowly behind him. The jungle path between Cuzacal and Tikal takes longer than ever before. No one speaks as they travel, though Itzel and Aapo exchange looks of annoyance over their agonizing pace. They have seen crippled turtles move faster. Nor does the pace quicken when they reach the city's boundaries. Every time they pass a doorway, the children pray they will turn inside, and their journey will be over.

Onward Itzel's grandfather leads them. Eventually, they come to the temple district. Tall pyramids, built with great, gray slabs of stone, tower over and around them. Itzel has been here before, and she feels humbled—even ashamed—by the sacred structures staring down at her.

"Grandfather, where are we going?" Itzel asks impatiently.

The old man points to the top of the highest pyramid and answers, "Up there."

The children share expressions of horror. Will her grandfather even survive a climb to the top? If so, how long will it take him? Itzel doesn't want to walk back through the jungle in darkness. There are too many terrors which dwell beneath night's shadow.

To her surprise, the old man climbs the steps as easily as he walks across even ground. But the sun is hot, and the stairs are long. By the time they reach the top, it is the children who are panting and exhausted, while Itzel's grandfather breathes evenly.

Here at the temple's summit, they find themselves face to face with a dark doorway. They have only seen priests enter this place, for the common people are forbidden from doing so.

"Why are we here?" Itzel asks, stepping to her grandfather's side.

"This," the old man answers, "is my home. I have lived here for many years."

The sun must have scrambled his mind! thinks Itzel. *He has been wandering the jungle for years and only now found his way out. Only a crazy man would call this place home.*

"Follow me," he instructs, stepping into shadow.

The chamber inside has a perfectly square floor with a vaulted ceiling above. There is a torch on the wall just inside the doorway. Its flame is barely flickering, ready to die. The old man picks up the torch and walks around the room with it. As he does, he lights a dozen more torches, all of which burn more brightly than the first. Soon the room is no longer dark, for it is awash in the red-orange glow of firelight.

Itzel no longer thinks her grandfather is crazy. It certainly does look like somebody lives here. There is a bed and clothing, a wash basin and table. Most notable and strange are the shelves. They are not filled with the normal trappings of everyday life: pottery, tools, baskets, and other items of that sort. Instead, they contain odd, rectangular objects unlike anything Itzel has ever seen.

"Please, forgive me," her grandfather says with a faint grin, "but I must lie down. It is how I spend most of my days. I am growing old and ill."

The old man stretches upon his mattress. Lying flat on his back, he turns his head to face them.

Itzel and Aapo approach the shelves, curious to sneak a better look at the boxy rectangles. They are threadbare and appear quite ancient. Itzel reaches out and strokes one with her fingertips.

"*Nimam*, what are these?" Itzel asks, her eyes and voice abounding with wonder.

"Those are called *books*, little Itzel," her grandfather replies. "They are filled with words. Thousands and thousands of words. Words from strange and distant tongues."

"What do the words say?" asks Aapo.

"They tell of a story," the old man answers. "A story of infinite importance for our world. A story that has been told and retold, written and rewritten, over and over again. It is the story I have guarded these many years. The story guarded by countless others before me, stretching all the way back to the foundations of the world itself."

Itzel and Aapo glance at each other. Both mouths hang open as they wonder what kind of story would be guarded so long and so secretively.

The old man continues. "But my time will soon be over. I do not have long before I will join my ancestors. I thought the secrets here would die with me. Then the gods sent me you, Itzel. Before I die, I must teach you many things. Then, when I am gone, you shall be the guardian of this place. You will be called the Keeper of Time."

"The Keeper of Time?" Itzel repeats. "What does that mean?"

"It means you will read and memorize every detail in those books. Then, even if the books are destroyed, you will hold them within your memory."

"Memorize all of *that?*" Itzel says skeptically. "No one can do such a thing!"

"I did such a thing!" her grandfather replies. "If I did, you will too. Besides, there is no option. If you don't, our world—our universe— cannot go on. All will be doomed to repeat itself once more."

"How can words have such importance, Grandfather?" Itzel asks, more disbelieving than ever.

"You will understand once you have read them," he replies. "But hear me now, little Itzel. There is no more important work in all the world than this task I give you today. Will you accept it?"

Itzel stares into the old man's pleading eyes, and she sees there is nothing crazy in them. She is certain that every word he has spoken is truth.

"Yes," she answers. "I will accept it."

"Good," he replies. Closing his eyes, he sighs with relief, as if she has quieted every fear in his old bones.

"What will I do with this knowledge?" asks Itzel. "What will I do as the Keeper of Time?"

"There is a day in the future when someone will come to this place," he answers, grabbing her hand. "It may not be during your lifetime. It may not happen yet for many lifetimes. But when this one comes, you must do everything in your power to help her succeed. Without you, and without your knowledge, everything is doomed to fail all over again."

"But how will I know who she is?" wonders Itzel. "How will I tell her apart from all the others?"

Her grandfather says nothing. He reaches into a pocket sewn inside his robe. When he removes his hand, there is a thin, curled-up slip of paper between his fingers.

"The girl in the middle," he says. "This is she. This is the One Who Mends Time Again."

Itzel takes the paper and unrolls it. Inside, there is a drawing. Its details are so fine, it looks real. Itzel feels like she is staring directly at the strangely dressed family, frozen in time. On one side stands a woman, a man on the other. Between them are two younger boys.

And, in the very middle, a smiling girl with hazel eyes and golden-brown hair.

An arrow points up at this girl from the bottom of the page. Below it are two words—words which Itzel cannot read yet, but which she will learn very well in time:

SOPHIA FARADAY

Afterword

ETTORE MAJORANA

Ettore Majorana is the only character in *The Slip through Time* based on a historical figure. There really was a gifted Italian theoretical physicist by this name, who also vanished under mysterious circumstances on March 25, 1938. One of his last known actions was to purchase a boat ticket from Palermo to Naples.

Beyond these few touchpoints of historical basis, however, the character Ettore in this story is fictional. There is absolutely no evidence that the real Majorana stole anybody's work and claimed it as his own, nor that he broke into the Vatican's archives to steal an ancient treasure. That he did so in *The Slip through Time* is purely dramatic license taken by the author in the telling of this story.

THE GEOGRAPHICAL SETTINGS

From Arches National Park in Utah to the Látrabjarg Bird Cliffs of Iceland, many of the locations Sophia visits in *The Slip through Time* are real places. While they may be filled with breathtaking scenery and important cultural history, they certainly do *not* contain the ancient pieces of a time machine.

If you ever have the opportunity to visit any of these places, please treat them with the respect they deserve. Obey all signs and rules posted by park or museum staff. By doing so, you can help to ensure not only your own safety, but also the enjoyment of these treasured places for future generations!

USAGE OF ANCIENT MAYAN LANGUAGES

The ancient Mayans of Mesoamerica did not speak one united language. Rather, there were dozens of different vocabularies and dialects used throughout the region. For the purposes of this book, the author opted to use the Classic Maya (or Ch'olti') language in the telling of Itzel's portion of the story. In a couple instances, for the sake of clarity, vocables from other dialects of the region were employed so as not to cause confusion for the reader.

 DENALI MAJESTO spent his earlier years in the private business sector, yet he never felt quite at home in what he was doing. After an early retirement from the world of business, Majesto dedicated his life to the three activities he treasures most: loving his family, exploring the globe, and writing. He has since written a small library's worth of stories, which he has begun unveiling to the world—one story at a time. Through both his writing and the tireless work of his ambassadors, it is Majesto's wish that he might entertain and bring hope to the lives of countless others.

To learn more about the man behind the stories, or to view his free content, please visit www.DenaliMajesto.com.

HIS STORIES ~ OUR LIBRARY

www.DenaliMajesto.com

Made in the USA
Monee, IL
30 July 2024

62809066R00142